"You think your uncle is going to be wowed by gingerbread and gumdrops?"

"I am fairly certain that Randall has never been in a baking competition and the man hates the taste of gingerbread," laughed Holly. "We've always made our gingerbread men out of sugar cookie dough because of him."

"Can you call them gingerbread men if they're made out of sugar cookie dough?"

"Loosen up, Jonah. Call a sugar cookie man a gingerbread man. It's okay. The gingerbread men of the world will not come after you with little gingerbread pitchforks if you let it slide."

Jonah snorted. "Tiny gingerbread pitchforks?" The image of gingerbread men with pitchforks chasing him around the house made him giggle.

Holly smirked. "I'm funny. I told you this."

She *was* funny. And beautiful. And a Hayward.

He couldn't forget their entire reason for being together was to keep their families apart. And she was *not* going to charm her way into his heart like her uncle had done to Gran...

Dear Reader,

I was so excited to write a Christmas book—and a Christmas wedding at that! Of course, I needed to stop that wedding since that's the name of the miniseries and all. Thankfully, even though my characters are a bit duplicitous, I get to teach them that it's never too late to get off Santa's naughty list and on his good one.

When Jonah's grandmother and Holly's great-uncle decide to get married, they can't begin to understand how that will ever work. Their two families will never get along, not to mention the two lovebirds are completely incompatible. What better way to show them this is a bad idea than to make them spend time together during their families' very different Christmas traditions—like a gingerbread house decorating contest and a winter rodeo?

These two might think their plan is perfect, but they start to enjoy each other's company more than they expected. Holly and Jonah have some hurdles to overcome. Let's hope a little Christmas spirit can do just that!

I love to connect with my readers on Facebook and Twitter: Facebook.com/amyvastineauthor and @vastine7. You can also sign up for my newsletter at amyvastine.com. Hope to see you there!

xoxo,

Amy

HEARTWARMING

The Christmas Wedding Crashers

—

Amy Vastine

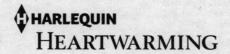

HARLEQUIN
HEARTWARMING

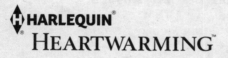

HARLEQUIN®
HEARTWARMING™

ISBN-13: 978-1-335-58475-5

The Christmas Wedding Crashers

Copyright © 2022 by Amy Vastine

Recycling programs for this product may not exist in your area.

This is a work of fiction. Names, characters, places and incidents are either the product of the author's imagination or are used fictitiously. Any resemblance to actual persons, living or dead, businesses, companies, events or locales is entirely coincidental.

For questions and comments about the quality of this book, please contact us at CustomerService@Harlequin.com.

Harlequin Enterprises ULC
22 Adelaide St. West, 41st Floor
Toronto, Ontario M5H 4E3, Canada
www.Harlequin.com

Printed in U.S.A.

Amy Vastine has been plotting stories in her head for as long as she can remember. An eternal optimist, she studied social work, hoping to teach others how to find their silver lining. Now she enjoys creating happily-ever-afters for all to read. Amy lives outside Chicago with her high-school-sweetheart husband, three teenagers who keep her on her toes and their two sweet but mischievous pups. Visit her at amyvastine.com.

Books by Amy Vastine

Harlequin Heartwarming

Stop the Wedding!

A Bridesmaid to Remember
His Brother's Bride
A Marriage of Inconvenience
The Sheriff's Valentine

Return of the Blackwell Brothers

The Rancher's Fake Fiancée

The Blackwell Sisters

Montana Wishes

Visit the Author Profile page
at Harlequin.com for more titles.

To all my amazing work friends—you know who you are and you know that I would not have survived this past year without you!

CHAPTER ONE

"IS IT TRUE? Did that old son of a gun strike it rich?"

Holly Hayward tipped the pint glass in her hand 45 degrees and pulled open the tap. Everyone's disbelief was understandable. Even she was having a hard time wrapping her head around this one. She straightened the glass and shut off the tap as soon as the foam reached the rim. "Would I be handing you a free glass of beer if he didn't?"

Thomas Maguire's muddy brown eyes were as round as the lotto balls that had made her great-uncle Randall a millionaire. "I can't believe it," he said, putting the glass to his lips and taking a little sip. "Is he paying every night from now on?"

Holly shook her head and wiped her hands on the apron tied around her waist. "Dream on, Tommy Boy. This is a one-day-only event here at the Roadrunner. Enjoy it while it lasts."

Thomas took another swig from his free drink and headed over to Uncle Randall's table to offer his thanks and congratulations. Randall was surrounded by his crew—Howie, his brother-in-law; Frank, his nephew; and Old Red, his best friend. The four of them could often be found sitting at that back table several nights a week, playing cards and laughing at something one of them said. Today, Randall decided he was extending their Thursday afternoon happy hour by paying for everyone's drinks the rest of the day.

"I don't know, Holly. This could force you Haywards to clean up your act," Josh Harvard said, bellying up to the bar. He was a regular and worked as a ranch hand at one of the largest ranches in town. "You'll be hobnobbing with the Coyote elite in no time."

There were two different kinds of people in Coyote, Colorado—the haves and the have-nots. Generation after generation, the Haywards had never been considered the former. They'd never been wealthy landowners or the kind of people who sought a vocation that required a college degree. Their bank accounts sometimes barely held enough to cover their expenses for the month. Randall's windfall was definitely going to change that, but not who they were as people.

Holly pushed her dark hair behind her shoulders. "I don't know about that. We Haywards prefer hanging out with the dregs of society like you," she teased. "They're so much more entertaining."

Josh laughed and wagged a finger at her. "That's not what you said when I asked you out last month."

"There's a big difference between hanging out with someone and dating that person. A woman has to have some standards, Josh. Did you even shower before coming out to-night? You look like you just finished muck-ing the stalls over there at the Starlight."

Josh readjusted the cowboy hat on his head and stared down at his outfit. His jeans were filthy and there was a piece of hay stuck to his plaid flannel sleeve. "What? I changed my boots and hat. I also washed my hands," he said, holding them up as proof.

Holly scrunched her face up in disgust.

Shaking her head, she muttered, "Never in all my life..." She poured him a beer and shooed him away from the bar.

Finding love in this town wasn't easy. Holly had pretty much given up. She was thirty years old and prepared to grow old alone. Her younger sister, Maisy, had a husband and two kids. Convincing herself that being the coolest aunt ever could be as satisfying as being someone's mom had become Holly's newest pastime. Uncle Randall had never married. He'd filled his life with his extended family and the friends he adored. Holly wouldn't mind being just like him. There were worse things to be.

"Can I get two more pitchers for table seven?" Maisy also worked at the Roadrunner. Holly didn't know how she did it. The woman stayed home all day with the kids while her husband worked his day job, then she came in and did an evening shift at the family bar and grill.

"Coming right up."

Maisy tightened her honey-colored ponytail and glanced around the bar. The Roadrunner was quite the hole-in-the-wall. There was a small dance floor, one pool table and a dozen tables scattered around them. Now that Thanksgiving had passed, Holly had begun Christmastizing it. A crooked, half-decorated tree stood in the corner and garland was strung above the bar. Maisy had helped her hang some gold cardboard stars from the ceiling with fishing line and duct tape.

"You know once word gets out that drinks are on Randall, there are going to be a million people in here," Maisy said.

"That means a million people will also be here to buy some food and that means more tips for you and me," Holly replied, trying to focus on the positive.

"We can hope."

Holly finished filling the pitchers and set them in front of her sister. She glanced over at their great-uncle. His eyes were glued to the entrance. There was a look of anticipation on his face as a large group entered. His face fell. Must not have seen whom he was hoping for. "I wonder who he's waiting for. He's been checking the door constantly."

Maisy swung her head around to see what Holly was talking about. She shrugged her shoulders. "I don't know. Maybe he's thinking what I'm thinking and realizes we're going to be slammed soon. Not sure he thought this drinks-on-me-tonight thing all the way through."

"Very true," Holly said with a laugh. Uncle Randall was more of an act-now-think-about-the-consequences-later kind of guy.

Holly and Maisy's dad pushed through the swinging door that led to the kitchen and his office in the back. Will Hayward was tall but wiry. What he lacked for hair on top of his head, he made up for with the bushiest beard on this side of the Rocky Mountains.

"How are things going out here?" he asked.

"So far so good," Holly replied, adding the pitchers of beer to Randall's tab. "Hope Uncle Randall is ready to become the most popular guy in town. Everyone wants to be a rich man's friend. Especially if that rich man buys them things."

"I've never met a rich and generous guy I didn't like." Her dad checked to make sure there were cut lemons for garnishes. "Of course, in this town, *rich* and *generous* are two adjectives that don't usually go together."

"Ain't that the truth!" Maisy said as she walked away with the drinks for Table Seven.

Three new people bellied up to the bar. Holly shooed her dad back to the kitchen. "We've got things handled out here. You make sure things keep running smooth in the back."

Will didn't move. His gaze was fixed on the front door. "What in the world is she doing here?"

Holly sidestepped to see around the head of the new customer at the bar and spotted Clarissa Drake standing awkwardly up front. Clarissa was the matriarch of the Drake family. Drakes did not come to the Roadrunner. Ever.

Almost twenty years ago, Connor Drake, Clarissa's husband, passed away, leaving behind his ranch for her to run. Their eldest son and daughter-in-law moved to Coyote to help, bringing along their son, Jonah. Jonah Drake was Holly's age. They had been twelve years old when he'd come to town. He might have been a cute kid, but the Haywards and the Drakes had a long-standing family feud that started with Holly's and

Jonah's great-grandfathers. There had been no chance Holly and Jonah could ever have been friends.

"She looks like she knows this is enemy territory," Holly observed with a smirk. "You think she thought someone with the last name Drake could get a free drink today?"

"Uh-oh, guess Randall is going to take care of this," Will replied.

Uncle Randall was headed right for her—he definitely appeared to be a man on a mission. Only, as soon as Clarissa spotted him, her entire face lit up. Holly was a bit taken aback.

"Can we get some drinks?" one of the men at the bar asked her.

She was quick to shush him as her brows pinched together. Uncle Randall *hugged* Clarissa Drake, then put his hand on the small of her back and ushered her to a private table.

"What is happening?" Will asked, clearly as flabbergasted as Holly.

"I… I don't know."

"Since when does Randall talk to Clarissa Drake?" Will put both hands on the bar as though he needed help keeping upright. "He hated Connor Drake. Connor Drake hated him."

"We plan to tip even though the drinks are free," the customer sitting across from them said.

Holly and her dad both hushed him. "Shh!"

Randall had hold of Clarissa's hand, and whatever he said to her put a smile on her face that went from ear to ear. Holly's gaze shifted from her uncle to her dad and back to her uncle. Randall was suddenly down on one knee.

"What is happening?" Will asked again.

"He's… He can't. What is he thinking?" Holly watched in utter horror as Randall pulled something out of his pocket that very much seemed to be a ring box. He opened it and Clarissa covered her mouth with her hand.

"Is he?" Will obviously couldn't say it aloud.

Clarissa wiped what must have been tears as she nodded her head. Randall put the ring on her finger. Holly was living in an upside-down world where her uncle just asked a Drake to marry him.

That was never happening. Only who was going to tell Uncle Randall that?

"OH, SHE'S SPITTING. She's spitting!" Dr. Jonah Drake announced.

"Sally's spitting!" Regina Butters and her daughter hugged as they hopped up and down in celebration. "We're going to have a baby!" they chanted in unison.

Baby llamas were actually called cria, but he wasn't going to correct them. They were finally going to have a cria. Jonah had been out to the Butters Farm three times since they had introduced a male into the harem in hopes that he could confirm at least one of their female llamas had been impregnated. Sally was the first one to pass the spit test, which was the inexpensive way for them to find out if they had a pregnant female. A spitting female meant she wasn't interested in mating anymore because she was already expecting.

"Congratulations," Jonah said, checking his watch. The sun was setting and this was his last stop of the day. He was ready to go home, clean up and feed his empty stomach.

He was about to enter some notes into his

phone when it began to ring with a call from the office. He answered it, concerned that it was an emergency call. An emergency meant his day could be far from finished.

"Hey, Jonah." It was Mandy, his receptionist. "I just got a strange call from Holly Hayward."

"Holly Hayward?" That didn't make sense. Holly had never called him. Drakes and Haywards didn't associate. It was the rule here in Coyote.

"She would like you to call her immediately. I have the number—should I text it to you?"

"Did she say what this is about? I don't recall the Haywards having any kind of animal they'd need my help with. You sure she didn't want Dr. Lang to call back?" Dr. Lang was Jonah's partner at the clinic and was in charge of the companion animals—the dogs and cats of Coyote.

"All she said was it was an emergency and she needs you to call her immediately. She was very specific about it being you."

As much as Jonah felt like blowing her off and going home, he was mildly curious about what would prompt Holly to reach out to him of all people during an emergency.

Mandy texted him the number and Jonah waited to call until he was finished up with Mrs. Butters. Once he was in his truck, he dialed Holly's number. She picked up almost immediately.

"Hello?"

"Um." Jonah was caught off guard with how promptly she'd answered. "Hey, this is Jonah... Jonah Drake. I got a message that you called..."

"You need to come to the Roadrunner right now and pick up your grandmother. I don't know what is going on, but if you all think that for one second my family and I are going to let your grandmother just weasel her way into my uncle's fortune, you are kidding yourself."

Jonah had absolutely no idea what she was talking about. Gran had a very tight group of friends who did things like play bridge at the social club. It did not include the likes of Randall Hayward or anyone in his circle. "My grandmother is at your bar right now?"

"Why else would I ask you to come pick her up?"

He ignored her lack of manners. "How did she get there?"

"She probably drove herself. I don't know!" Holly sounded exasperated. She should've tried being on his side of the call.

"Is she intoxicated? Can she not drive herself home?"

"I'm not serving your grandmother! I just need you to come get her. This is not happening. I don't know if you're in on this or what, but it is not happening."

Jonah's head began to hurt more than his stomach. He had basically lived under his grandmother's roof since he was twelve. Never in all those years had she ever gone out to a bar and she'd never associated with anyone from the Hayward family. Drakes and Haywards had a rivalry that had begun long before Jonah's father was even born.

"I don't understand what you're saying, Holly. Is my grandma okay?" A bit of worry began to creep into the back of his mind. He put the call on speaker and started to text his mother. Maybe she knew why Gran was hanging out at the Roadrunner, causing Holly to melt down.

Jonah had felt responsible for taking care

of his mother and his grandmother after his father had passed away the same year Jonah finished veterinary school. He had thought he was about to start a new life away from Coyote, Colorado, but instead he was dragged right back to the ranch.

"Let's just say it's a bit suspicious that as soon as my uncle Randall hits it big in the lottery, your grandmother is over here trying to get her piece."

Trying to get her piece? There was no reason for Gran to want a piece of his winnings. The ranch provided for her just fine.

Jonah had heard that Randall Hayward had won himself some money. It was big news in town. He'd bought a lottery ticket at the little gas station on the corner of Main and Hilton Street. It was a big deal for a guy who had spent his life working in the rodeo. He had been some kind of rodeo clown. Another reason it didn't make sense that his grandmother was there. She hated the rodeo.

"I'll be there in ten minutes. Whatever you think she's doing, she's probably not doing. Please don't be mean to her."

Holly had the audacity to sound offended. "I'm not going to be mean to her. And she is definitely doing what I think she is doing. I want you to get her out of my bar."

Holly had been mean to Jonah since the moment she met him. It didn't matter that he had no idea who she was or who her family was when he first got to town. She had been rude from the get-go. On his first day of school, she'd kicked him in the shin for no reason and stuck bubble gum on his chair, which, thankfully, he noticed before he had sat down.

"Trust me, I don't want her anywhere near you or yours. I'll be there in…nine minutes."

Eight minutes later, Jonah pulled up to the Roadrunner. The small parking lot was crammed full of cars. There wasn't one open spot. Since he had no intention of staying longer than it would take to get his grandmother out of the place, he parked his truck right out front.

His mother had been completely unaware of what Gran was up to. She had told her she was dropping off a cross-stitch to a friend. Jonah feared the worst. Gran had always been so proud of the fact that her age may have slowed down her body, but it hadn't gotten her mind. She was sharp as a tack.

He prayed time wasn't taking its toll on that as well.

When he stepped inside the Haywards' establishment, it was loud and crowded. The smell of beer was in the air and the floor was a little sticky. Jonah was glad he had on his work boots and not his good shoes. This place was sure to leave its mark.

Jonah finally spotted his grandmother sitting at a table in the corner, holding a champagne flute. So much for Holly's assertion that she wasn't going to serve her.

"Good, you're here." Speak of the devil, there was Holly Hayward standing right in front of him. It bothered him that every time he saw her, she seemed to get more beautiful. It didn't take long, however, for that to be overshadowed by her caustic personality. "Now, go over there and get your grandmother."

"That's what I'm trying to do if you'd please get out of my way so I can continue moving in that direction." He waited for her to move.

"Jeez, you don't have to be rude about it," she huffed but stepped aside.

"Rude? I'm being rude? You are the blackest kettle in all of Pot Land, Hayward."

Her forehead creased. "What does that mean? You know what, I don't care. Just go over there and get her out of here."

Jonah tried taking a deep breath and counting to five. He was not going to let this woman get under his skin with her abrasiveness. He calmed his temper and weaved his way over to his grandmother.

"Gran," he said when he got close enough.

His grandmother's eyes went wide with surprise. She quickly set down her champagne and stood. "Jonah, what are you doing here?"

"What am I doing here? What are you doing here? This bar is owned by the Haywards, Gran. We shouldn't be here. Let me take you home, okay?"

Gran didn't move, however. She actually sat back down and glanced across the table at the man seated there. Jonah quickly realized it was Randall Hayward. The old man turned his body and looked up at Jonah.

"Hey, why don't you sit with us for a minute?" he suggested. "Can I buy you a drink?

I'm buying everyone a drink. What would you like? Anything at all, it's on the house."

"I don't want a drink, Mr. Hayward. I want to take my grandmother home. She is clearly unaware of what is going on here. I need to get her home."

"I am fully aware of what is going on, Jonah," his grandmother asserted. "Sit down."

Jonah had been born a rule follower. When his grandmother told him to do something, he did it. He took the seat next to her.

"I've wanted to talk to you about something for a little bit now," Gran said. "I just couldn't figure out how to start the conversation, but things have changed in a way that makes it impossible for me to hide things from you or the rest of the family any longer."

"Wouldn't it be better if you, me and Mom had this conversation together back at home, then?"

"I think it's best if you hear it now. Then you can help me break the news to your mom and your uncle. Oliver is not going to take this news well."

"I don't know if a crowded public place is

the best setting for a serious conversation," Jonah said, hoping she'd concede.

"Jonah, I've asked your grandmother to marry me and she said yes," Randall said matter-of-factly.

It was as if every other person in this sticky, smelly, noisy place disappeared. The only ones Jonah could see were his grandmother and Randall.

"You did what?"

"I know this seems a little strange since you had no idea that Randall and I were dating, but we have been together now for over a month." Gran's hands were moving at lightning speed. She always talked with her hands when she was nervous.

"You've been dating for over a month? *You and Randall Hayward?*"

"My family is just as surprised as you are. They had no idea either, and I am sure my nephew is in the kitchen trying to figure out how to kick all these people out so he can read me the riot act."

Jonah didn't know about Will Hayward but Holly was hot enough for both of them. This was the emergency. How had she failed to tell him that her scoundrel of an uncle was trying to seduce his poor grandmother? That seemed like an important detail she left out of their phone conversation.

"Can you two excuse me for a second? I think I need that drink." Jonah rose to his feet and made a beeline for the bar, where Holly was watching intently.

"What are you doing? I asked you to take your grandmother home, not sit down and have a chat with them," she snapped as soon as he sat on an empty stool.

"Maybe you could have mentioned the whole engagement thing when you called me." It felt like he had steam coming out of his ears.

Again, she seemed offended. "I'm pretty sure I did."

"Uh, no, you did not."

"I told you that we weren't going to allow your grandmother to take advantage of my uncle just because she wants his money."

Jonah's hackles were raised. "Take advantage of your uncle? You think this is about my sweet grandmother taking advantage of your con man of an uncle? Are you kidding me right now?"

"Con man? Uncle Randall is a respected member of this community."

Jonah couldn't help but laugh.

Holly narrowed her eyes and her jaw was tight. "He has more friends than everyone in your family combined."

"*Friends?* I couldn't care less about how many friends someone has. Maybe he should go ask one of those friends of his to marry him. Not my grandmother. He needs to forget about my gran and stick with the friends he's had longer than a month!"

"They've been dating for a month?"

"Only a month." Jonah pinched the bridge of his nose. How in the world could this have been going on under his nose for the last month?

"My family is not going to be in support of this wedding."

"As if my family will be? My grandfather and your uncle were not friends. Your uncle over there and your grandfather used to make trouble on our ranch. My dad used to tell me stories about how you Haywards only knew how to wreck things. Vandals and thieves. That's what he used to call you all."

"Funny, I heard your grandfather was a real stick-in-the-mud. I also heard he was a big-time liar and don't get me started on how arrogant he was."

She wasn't going to goad him into a fight. It wasn't worth his time to try to argue with her. "Well, I guess we both feel very strongly about the fact that our two families should never mingle. I will handle things with my grandmother and you need to make sure you keep your uncle and all his money away from her."

Holly had her arms crossed in front of her chest and a scowl on that pretty face of hers. "Fine. I don't want to see her in my bar again."

"I don't know why she would ever want to be here. This place needs to be sprayed down with a few gallons of bleach. I can't believe you aren't violating some health codes."

"Oh, I'm sorry this isn't a prim-and-proper place where you can canoodle with your fancy friends."

"*Canoodle*. That's a big word for you."

"You can leave now." She pointed at the door.

Jonah stood up. That was a low blow and

he knew it. "I'm leaving. I just need to know one thing. Why did you call me?"

Holly scratched the back of her head and her gaze dropped to the floor. "You're smart, Jonah. You've always been the smartest guy in the room. I figured if anyone could stop this from happening, it was you."

That was…unexpected. Did Holly Hayward just compliment him? It seemed to pain her to admit it, so maybe it was for real.

"I'm going to do my best."

Holly gave him a nod. Now, he had to figure out how to convince his gran to leave with him.

CHAPTER TWO

HOLLY WATCHED AS Jonah went back over to his grandmother and pleaded with her to leave with him. The old woman would not relent, and Jonah ended up sitting with them as many others came over to offer congratulations to the engaged couple.

Holly had to give it to Jonah. She certainly could not sit there quietly. He could have left, as it was likely that his grandmother had driven herself there. He probably did not trust that she wouldn't be harassed. Of course, no Hayward would go near them. Will had retreated to the kitchen and Maisy stuck to the other side of the bar. Holly kept bartending.

Finally, Clarissa stood. Holly cringed as the older woman gave Randall a kiss before she and Jonah left. Could Randall really be in love with a Drake? He had always been very clear about how he felt about that family. It was always ironic that the Drakes called the Haywards thieves and liars when they were the ones who had stolen from Holly's great-grandfather.

Will came bursting out of the back. "I'm going to tell them she has to leave."

Holly chased after him and tugged on the back of his shirt. "She's gone. I had Jonah come and get her."

"You did what?"

"He failed to convince her to leave, but it seems she doesn't stay out as late as our kind do. Why don't you calm down and go find out what Randall is thinking. You know he won't listen to us if you're too heated."

"Why do you think I went back to the kitchen? I've been calming down." His nostrils still flared.

"Dad." Holly would defend her family to the death, but she wasn't blind to the fact that they were sometimes ruled by their emotions. That didn't always end well.

"The Drakes stole my grandfather's land. They cheated our family out of what was rightfully ours. I don't know if Randall thinks by doing this, he can get our land back, but this can't be the way he does it."

Maisy appeared and put a hand on her dad's shoulder. "Please don't do anything that could cause Uncle Randall to leave without paying his bill for all the drinks we've been giving away tonight."

Randall would never do that, but Holly didn't want her dad to make a scene, either. "Whatever you're about to do, make sure you do it without getting angry," she begged her dad.

Will rolled his shoulders and took a deep breath. "I'm going to reason with him."

Maisy and Holly exchanged glances. Reason wasn't one of their father's strengths. All three of them marched over to Randall. Old Red, Frank, and Howie had moved over there after Clarissa and Jonah left.

"We need to talk," Will said.

Randall sighed deeply. "I should have told you Clarissa and I were spending time together. I didn't mean to shock you all, but love makes a man a fool sometimes."

"Love?" Will scoffed. "Uncle Randall, you can't possibly be in love with that woman. She was married to Connor Drake. I know you haven't forgotten what Connor and

Leonard Drake and their father did to our family."

"I have not. I will not. But Clarissa is not Connor."

"She's his widow," Will said, taking the seat that used to be occupied by Clarissa herself. "There's no way she wasn't aware of the man Connor was, and yet, she stood by him."

Randall rested his elbows on the table and laced his fingers together. "We can't live in the past, William. At some point, we need to enjoy the present."

Will seemed at a loss for words. Holly wasn't sure what to say, either. This grudge was in their blood. She didn't know who they were without it.

Frank sided with his cousin. "You can't tell Will not to live in the past when we were basically raised to hate anyone with the last name Drake. You, Uncle Scott, Mom, Grandpa—you all made it clear that we should never trust a Drake."

"She was only a Drake by marriage," Randall tried to rationalize.

"I, for one, am happy to hear my dear brother-in-law is finally going to settle down," Howie said, earning him a dirty look from Will and Frank.

Will tried to reason with his uncle. "I get that she's only a Drake by marriage, but you marry her, you marry into her family. Her kids are Drakes through and through. I, for one, do not want to associate with the likes of Oliver Drake."

"Why do you have to marry her?" Holly asked. "You've been happy dating all these years without settling down. Why would you change all that for her?"

Randall was hearing none of it. "She's the one, sweetheart." His expression turned wistful. "When you meet the one, you don't just date her."

Maisy put a hand over her heart. "That is the most romantic thing I've heard in a long time."

"You're not helping, Maisy," their dad complained. "Get back to work if you aren't going to help us talk him out of this."

"There's no talking me out of this. I have lived alone my whole life. I finally have a chance to share it with someone."

Old Red was Randall's oldest and best friend. "You finally have the money you need to do anything you want and you want to tie yourself down to one woman?"

"When that woman is as amazing as my Clarissa, I'm happy to be tied down. The money I won is just the cherry on top."

It was the second time today that Holly felt like her world was being turned upside down. Randall was too enamored to be swayed tonight. Anything they said would be wasted breath.

"Aw, come on you guys. How can you not see how romantic this is?" Maisy asked. She gave Uncle Randall a kiss on the cheek. "Congratulations, Uncle. If no one else is going to be happy for you, I will."

Will smacked himself on the forehead and Holly tugged her sister away. "We need to get back to work," she said.

"Maybe it's time for us to get over this family feud. If Uncle Randall can stop holding a grudge against someone with the last name Drake, I think we all can."

"Just like that? You can let it all go just like that?" Holly couldn't understand her sister's lack of family loyalty.

"Maybe because deep down I never really

had a reason to hate anyone," Maisy said with a shrug and walked away.

Holly stood there dumbfounded. How could that be? Had she not grown up in the same town? Surrounded by the same people? Aware of the same stories of the past? Like Frank had said, hating the Drakes was instilled in them from birth. For her entire life, they had acted as if they were better than anyone with the last name Hayward. Holly felt justified in standing by her father on this one.

Will rejoined her at the bar. "There's no reasoning with him."

"He's happy. We can't convince him this is a bad idea tonight. I think you should try again tomorrow."

Someone at the bar spilled what was left of their drink and Will grabbed a towel to clean it up. "I don't know if I am the right person to do it. He thinks that I'm the one being stubborn while he's nothing but a love-struck fool."

Love made people do things against their better judgment. Holly had seen it one too many times. "I don't know if we can convince him he's wrong. I think we need him to come to that conclusion on his own."

"He wants to get married on Christmas! I don't know if we have the time to sit by and wait for him to come to his senses."

Holly couldn't understand why the rush. Christmas was only a few weeks away. How could she possibly help her uncle overcome the bliss that had fogged his memory with only a little over three weeks to work with?

"I promise I will find a way to stop this wedding from happening."

"I hope so. My father would be beside himself if he were alive to see this. The Drake family has taken enough from us. They can't have Randall." Will grabbed a tray of dirty glasses and headed back into the kitchen.

Holly would come up with a plan that would make her grandfather proud. As long as Clarissa's family didn't welcome Randall with open arms, it should be easy to convince Randall it wasn't going to work. The two families would never get along. It wasn't just the feud. They were polar opposites in every way.

Until Uncle Randall got rich.

Jonah didn't seem swayed by Randall's newfound wealth, but would all the Drakes feel the same way? Randall's money changed things. The rich always wanted to get richer.

Connor and Clarissa had had two sons—Jonah's dad and his uncle Oliver. Jonah's dad had passed away years ago, but Oliver Drake was one of the wealthiest people in Coyote. While his brother had run the family ranch, Oliver branched out and owned four car dealerships in the area. Everyone in Coyote except the Haywards bought their cars and trucks from a Drake dealership.

Oliver might love getting his hands on some of Randall's lottery winnings. Holly would have to touch base with Jonah one more time to be assured they were all on the same page. There would be no Hayward-Drake Christmas wedding.

"A Christmas wedding?" Uncle Oliver was not taking the news well.

Jonah's phone lay on the kitchen table on speaker. His grandmother sat across from him and his mother next to him.

"I'm happy, Oliver. Can't you be happy for me?" Clarissa asked.

"Mom." Oliver took a deep breath. "Of course I want you to be happy, but I don't understand why you think that Randall Hayward can make you happy. The Haywards are not good people. They have been trash-talking our family for decades. They're a bunch of hooligans. Randall is the worst. How in the world did you get involved with someone like him? He certainly hasn't been hanging around church or the club."

Randall would probably burst into flames if he stepped inside a church. Jonah had to agree with his uncle. There were not two people less alike than his gran and Randall.

"We met at the Hen House. We both enjoy their Tuesday special—the Sunshine Breakfast. He was also kind enough to share his newspaper with me. One day he asked for my help with the crossword puzzle and the rest is history."

"You fell in love over a crossword puzzle and some eggs?" Oliver sounded flabbergasted.

Gran smiled like a love-struck teenager. "I know it sounds crazy, but he's not who you think he is."

"I think he's exactly who we think he is

and you have been tricked into thinking he's someone else because he knows how to be charming. Charisma is not the same as character," Jonah warned her.

"Jonah's right, Mom," Oliver said.

Jonah's mom had been silent thus far. He was sure she had some thoughts on this matter but was keeping them to herself for the time being. She would wait until Oliver was off the phone before she'd give her two cents.

"I know I can't convince you guys. I only hope that you'll give Randall a chance so he can prove to you that he's the man who can make me happy the rest of my days."

Oliver sighed so loudly that Jonah could feel the weight of his skepticism. It wouldn't matter how nice Randall was, Oliver would never believe he was good enough to be married to Gran.

"Why don't you give us some time?" Jonah asked, hoping she would at least see the benefit in that. "This Christmas is not enough time for us to get to know Randall."

"I've always loved Christmas, you know that. As soon as he asked me to marry him,

I couldn't think of a more perfect day to tie the knot."

Oliver's tone was still full of aggravation. "Okay, so what's wrong with planning a wedding for next Christmas? Why would you need to rush into things?"

"I don't know if you've noticed, but I'm not getting any younger. Time isn't on my side, sweetheart."

Jonah cocked his head to the side. "Gran, you have plenty of Christmases ahead of you."

Clarissa reached her hand across the table and placed it on Jonah's. "I hope so, but we aren't guaranteed anything. Putting off the things we know will make us happy is one of the most foolish things we can do."

"That's funny, because I was going to say getting married to your family's worst enemy is the most foolish thing you can do," Oliver replied.

"Hey, Uncle Oliver," Jonah said, picking up his phone. His grandmother had endured enough of his grief. "I think we all need to get some sleep. We can talk more about this tomorrow."

"Maybe a good night's sleep will help her come to her senses," Oliver grumbled.

Gran snatched the phone from Jonah. "Good night, dear," she said before pressing End. "That's enough of that. Let's hope that a good night's sleep will help him come to his senses. I am marrying Randall on Christmas."

Jonah glanced at his mom, who still sat silently. He didn't doubt his grandmother was determined to see this through. Convincing her that Randall Hayward was the wrong man for her was going to be difficult. Challenging but not impossible. A little sleep, a clear head and Jonah would figure out how to get things back to normal.

Clarissa wished Jonah and his mom a good night and went to get ready for bed. His mom folded her hands on the table. She slowly shook her head back and forth and pressed her lips together to fight a smile.

"You were awfully quiet," Jonah said, hoping she was ready to share her opinion.

"Your father would have been a thousand times angrier than Oliver is. The Haywards have never done anything but make trouble for our family. Who would have thought they'd cause the most trouble by trying to marry Gran?" She covered her mouth to muffle her laughter.

Jonah couldn't help but chuckle a little bit. This was so preposterous.

His mother tried to rein in her emotions. "Never in a million years would I have guessed this would be a problem we'd have to fix. You know me. I haven't dared disagree with your grandmother in all these years, and I will not start now. But... I fear your father's ghost will haunt us the rest of our days if she marries a Hayward. You and Oliver have got to stop this wedding."

Clearly it would have to be Jonah. Uncle Oliver was usually a superb salesman. He could convince perfect strangers they needed and wanted whatever car he decided they should buy. However, when it came to his mother, he tended to forget all of his smooth-talking ways. He often treated her like she wasn't capable of making her own decisions and, in this case, that attitude might just push her into the waiting arms of Mr. Hayward. Jonah needed to take another approach.

THE NEXT MORNING, Jonah wished he felt more prepared to have a conversation with his grandmother. She woke up ready to plan a dream Christmas wedding with his mother's assistance. Jonah went to work unclear what it would take to get this wedding at least postponed.

He parked his truck near his vet clinic and found Holly pacing outside the front door.

"Please tell me you're here to report that Randall has decided he can't marry my grandmother."

Her lack of enthusiasm told him that was not the case. "I was hoping you had convinced your grandmother to give back the ring after you left the Roadrunner."

Jonah pulled out his keys and unlocked the clinic door. "Randall has completely hoodwinked her into thinking he's the perfect man for her. It's going to take a lot more than me just saying it to convince her he's not."

"Well, your grandmother has also tricked my great-uncle into thinking she's the perfect woman for him even though it's obvious she's not." She followed him into the clinic. "So, what's the plan?"

"What do you mean what's the plan?"

Holly threw her hands up. "You have to have a plan."

"What about you? Why don't you have a plan?"

"Like I said last night, you're the smart one. I'm happy to help you put whatever you come up with into action."

Just what he needed. Although, it was helpful that Randall's family was as against this union as he was. "I don't have a plan yet. It's not as simple as reasoning with her. I have to get her to see that this is a bad idea all on her own."

"That's what I was thinking. Randall just needs a wake-up call. The two of them are not as compatible as they think they are."

Jonah flipped on some lights and set his bag on the reception desk. He finally took a good look at Holly. She had her hair pulled up in a messy ponytail and some dark circles under her eyes. On one foot was a brown boot and on the other was a black boot. Had she gotten ready in the dark?

"Are you okay?" Should he be concerned? Holly had always come across tough as nails. Nothing rattled her. She might have always been looking for a fight, but never actually looked like she'd just been in one.

Holly seemed caught off guard by his concern. She gave herself a once-over and noticed her mismatched boots. "Goodness, I'm having a morning," she said with a shake of her head. "This mess had me up all night. I just need some sleep. I'll sleep better if I know we're all working to the same end. All of you. Your uncle included."

Jonah laughed. "Trust me, no one was more displeased with the news of their engagement than my uncle."

"You didn't see how my dad took it," she replied with wide eyes.

To say Will and Oliver simply did not get along would be the understatement of the year. This could be the one thing the two of them would ever agree upon.

"We have to be careful how hard we push. It could just push them closer together."

Holly stepped closer. "That's what I said. We need to be gentle in our approach or it's not going to work."

It was strange to be on the same page. Growing up, Jonah often thought Holly did or said things just to be opposite of him. "I have a lot on my plate today. Then I have to take Gran to the tree-lighting ceremony tonight. Maybe we can meet there and talk strategy?"

"I haven't been to the tree-lighting ceremony since I was a little kid. Why don't you drop by the Roadrunner when you're done watching the mayor flip a switch."

"Since you were a little kid? It's the biggest Christmas event in Coyote."

"We have a bar to run. That's where I spend my evenings, where my dad has spent his evenings since I was born. You're welcome to come by."

Welcome wasn't exactly how he had felt last night when she invited him there. "I would prefer to meet on neutral ground. Maybe you could get off early or take a little break and meet me in the town square. I mean how busy is the bar going to be when practically the whole town is at the ceremony?"

Jonah took a step back because the look on Holly's face could quite possibly kill, but her expression quickly softened. She reached into her pocket, pulling out her phone.

"Fine. I'll meet you at the tree lighting.

Give me your number and I'll text you when I'm there. My time will be limited."

It was sort of unbelievable that he was giving his number to Holly. She had made it clear from the moment they met that the only thing she would have done with that information was prank call him. They were adults now. Surely she wouldn't still be doing childish things like that.

It was as if she read his mind while he hesitated. "It's not like I'm going to sell it on the dark web, Jonah. I'll delete it once we break up Randall and Clarissa. I promise." He rattled off the digits. She punched the numbers into her phone and slid it back into her pocket. "Okay, I'll text you later, then."

"I'll see you tonight."

She began to back away. Perhaps their alliance was just as unnerving for her as it was for him. This was about to get interesting.

CHAPTER THREE

IT WAS QUITE possible that the whole town was present for the tree-lighting ceremony. Holly weaved her way through the crowded sidewalk. The square was completely decked out for the holidays. All the streetlight poles were wrapped in garland and topped with giant red velvet bows. The leafless trees that lined the parkways were covered in hundreds of white twinkling lights. Wreaths hung by ribbons on the doors of the businesses all along the main drag, and in the center of it all was the 50-foot Christmas tree ready to light up the whole downtown.

It had been a long time since Holly had witnessed the annual tree lighting. She had loved coming down here with her mom and sister when she was little. They used to get hot chocolate with candy cane stirrers and joyfully shouted the countdown in unison with the rest of the Coyote community.

Holly had once dreamed she'd be the one who would flip the switch when she got older. That honor was only given to the mayor of Coyote. Being mayor was a childish fantasy for someone like Holly, though. Her reality was that once she had been old enough to bus tables, her dad had asked her to work at the Roadrunner.

People like Jonah got to be mayor. They went to college and were worldly about things like art and politics. They did things like read for pleasure. Holly wasn't and didn't do those things.

Meet you by the Knitting Needle.

That had been Jonah's reply when Holly texted him that she was there. She was across the street from their meetup spot when she saw him. He had on a black pea-coat, jeans and a bright red scarf around his neck. Holly could admit that he was good-looking. When he moved to town, all the girls had gone wild for him. Not only had he been cute, but he'd been smart and wealthy as well. There had been quite a few teenage girls who imagined being Mrs. Jonah Drake back in high school. Holly was not one of them, of course.

"Jonah," she said as she crossed the street and came up behind him.

He spun around and seemed surprised to see her. Of course, the last time he'd seen her she had been a hot mess. Holly wasn't even sure how she managed to put on two different boots this morning. Tonight, she looked normal.

"Looks like getting some rest did you some good," Jonah said, slipping both hands into his coat pockets.

"I have a much clearer head, thank you. I'm ready to brainstorm." She tried to say it with some confidence. Holly felt self-conscious about her smarts in front of Jonah. Always had. He was brilliant. Annoyingly so. He had been the guy who always knew the answer in school. The one everyone wanted to partner up with because they knew they'd get the best grade.

"Great. I don't know what you've come up with, but I have a plan that might work." He motioned toward the bench in front of Howler's Ice Cream. "Let's see which one sounds better."

Holly hesitated. Of course he had already come up with something. She had racked her brain all day and still wasn't sure what to do.

Jonah sat down and patted the empty spot next to him. "My patients bite. I don't."

Holly wanted to knock that charming grin off his face. She wasn't afraid of him. She sat down and crossed her legs. "Let's hear it."

"What if we staged an intervention? We could each gather all the people who love them and sit them down, separately of course, like people do with alcoholics and explain to them that they are headed down a dark path and that we love them and only want what's best."

Jonah had clearly never been to a real intervention. "Well, unless you plan to send your grandma to a spa in California for the next couple months, I don't think that's going to work. Interventions don't convince people to stop loving what's bad for them. It just gets them to agree to go somewhere they can't access what they love for a while."

Jonah thought about it for a second. "Well, what's your idea?"

"I don't have one. I said I was here to

brainstorm. I was hoping you'd get the ball rolling and I'd help tweak it. I can't tweak that intervention idea. It's not going to work. Period."

"Shooting down my idea by saying it just won't work isn't very helpful."

"We need them to figure it out. We need the breakup to be their idea." Of this, Holly was sure. "Neither one of them is going to listen to any of us. They already know we all hate this idea. I need Randall to wake up and see that he is never going to enjoy talking about needlepoint or hanging out at the social club playing dominoes. That's just not who he is."

"That's it!" Jonah hopped up to his feet. "I have to admit it, you're right."

Those were words Holly was not used to hearing coming out of Jonah's mouth. He was the guy who always had to be right. He usually was right, but that was beside the point.

"I'm right?"

"What kinds of things does Randall do this time of year?"

Holly wasn't sure what that meant. Randall didn't do things based on the time of year. "He does the same things he always does. Hang out with friends, drink at the Roadrunner."

"There have to be holiday things he likes to do this time of year. Like, my grandmother judges the gingerbread house contest at the Coyote Social Club and she wraps presents for needy families with the church."

"Randall doesn't have anything to do with the Coyote Social Club and he isn't much for buying gifts, never mind wrapping them. He's the kind of guy who hands each of the kids in the family five bucks and tells them not to spend it all in one place."

"See? Perfect!"

Even though this was Holly's idea, she had no clue what the actual plan was. "What does gingerbread and gift wrapping have to do with convincing these two they can't get married?"

"Instead of trying to break them apart, we're going to make them spend time together. Spending time together is the best way to get them to see how completely incompatible they are. It's brilliant."

Holly felt a rush of pride. It was kind of brilliant.

"So, I make Randall come to the ginger-bread contest and the gift-wrapping party and...oh! Randall and his friends always go to the Reindeer Rodeo over at Delany Arena this time of year. Does your grandmother like the rodeo?"

"Absolutely not," Jonah said with the biggest grin. "She hates it. My grandfather used to take my cousins and me but Gran never joined us. She loves horses and horse shows, but the rodeo was a little too wild for her."

"Then she really must come with us this year," Holly said with a waggle of her brows. Another thought popped in her head. "The Frontier Freeze. There's no way your grandma does the Frontier Freeze."

"The thing where people run into the icy-cold river? On purpose?"

Holly nodded her head. All of the Hay-wards had done the Frontier Freeze at least once in their lives. Randall and his crew did it every year. It was tradition. "Nothing makes you feel more alive than hypo-thermia."

Jonah seemed beyond pleased. He looked like a little kid who just got everything he wanted for Christmas, nearly bouncing with excitement. "I'm going to put you two on the list for the gingerbread contest. It's tomorrow at ten in the morning. Hopefully that doesn't interfere with your job."

His consideration caught Holly off guard. "I'm usually free Saturday mornings. I should be able to bring Randall."

"This is going to work."

"For sure. The Drakes and the Haywards have nothing in common except for the fact that we dislike one another. Randall will see that she is not the woman for him."

Jonah stilled. "Not before she sees he's not the man for her."

Holly got to her feet. She knew a challenge when she heard one. "Bet."

"Bet what?"

"Let's bet. I bet that Randall will come to his senses before Clarissa does."

Jonah chuckled, shaking his head. "I'm not betting you."

"Because you know you're going to lose. I get it."

"I am not afraid of losing. I just don't feel the need to turn everything into a competition like some people do."

Holly narrowed her eyes. "I do not need to turn everything into a competition."

He laughed harder. "Holly, you are the most competitive person I have ever met in my whole life."

She folded her arms across her chest. "I am not. You are the one who always has to be right. No one could possibly compete with you."

"Me?" Jonah pointed to his chest. "I am not the one who had to be captain every time we played a game in PE class. You were the one who would always stack her team so she never lost."

"Stack my team? Isn't that the whole point of choosing teams? To choose the best players so you win? You're the one who used to ask everyone around you how they did on the test just so you could inform them that you did better."

Jonah's jaw dropped. "I did not do that!"

"I was in several classes with you, Jonah Drake."

"Yeah, and I recall you asking me multiple times if I got a hundred percent just to embarrass me when I had to admit I didn't."

Holly had to think back. Honestly, she had

done that sometimes. If she hadn't given him the chance to brag, he would have taken it. "I wasn't trying to embarrass you. I was just beating you to the punch."

"Competitive. See?"

"Fine, I like to win and you like to be right. All I'm saying is let's make it fun. If Randall breaks things off, you have to advertise for the Roadrunner at your clinic."

"Oh, we're not betting for money?"

Holly waved that idea off. "Money bets are boring. That's like choosing a truth during a game of Truth or Dare. Dares are so much more exciting."

"Shocking that you would always go for the dare," he replied sarcastically. "Okay, if I lose, I'll advertise for the Roadrunner, but if my grandmother calls things off first, you have to wear a shirt to work once a week for the entire year that says, 'I lost to Jonah Drake.'"

"You think I'm going to publicly announce that I lost to you for an entire year?"

He tilted his head and that annoying grin was back. "Someone's afraid they aren't going to win, huh?"

Holly scrunched up her nose. "I am not

the least bit afraid of losing, so you could ask me to wear a shirt for the rest of my life and I'd take that bet because I am going to win."

"Shake on it." Jonah stuck out his hand.

Holly shook it without breaking eye contact. She let go and started to back away. "Text me all the activities your grandmother will be attending with dates and times. I'll do the same for Randall. We should get started as soon as possible."

"What about tonight?" Jonah asked, causing her to stop in her tracks. "Does he usually attend the tree lighting?"

"No, he's at the bar right now."

"Why don't you call him up and have him meet you here to spend some time with Gran and her family? We usually go ice-skating after the tree gets lit. How does Randall feel about being on the ice?"

The man was good. This was the best plan to stop this wedding from ever happening. "I'll call him."

JONAH REJOINED HIS family as they waited for the Christmas tree lighting. He couldn't help but smile at the thought of Holly and Randall joining them for ice-skating. He needed to explain his plan to his uncle before they showed up, though.

"Does anyone need a refill on hot chocolate before the mayor starts?" Jonah asked. His cousin Julia's three kids pleaded for more. "Perhaps you can come with me, Uncle Oliver? Help me carry the cups for your grandkids?"

Oliver eyed Jonah suspiciously but went along. As soon as they were away from Gran, Jonah filled him in on the plan.

"So you think that by acting like we have no issues with this and inviting this man to spend more time with your grandmother, she'll call things off?"

"You can still take issue with the wedding happening so soon. But I do think that by encouraging them to spend time together, they will come to the conclusion that this is not a match made in heaven."

Oliver wasn't sold. "That seems risky. What are the other ideas?"

"I don't have any other ideas at the moment. We've ruled out doing an intervention."

"Who's we?"

Jonah got in line for the hot chocolate.

The temperature had dropped and he rubbed his gloved hands together. "Me and Holly Hayward."

"You and Will Hayward's oldest daughter?" Uncle Oliver shook his head. "Why are you talking to the enemy?"

"Holly is not the enemy," Jonah said, earning himself a glare from his uncle. "I get it—you think all the Haywards are the enemy. Holly is trying to stop this wedding from happening as much as we are. She actually thinks you and Gran might be trying to get some of Randall's money."

"Ha!" Oliver's laugh was so loud it startled the woman in line in front of them.

Jonah apologized to her and lowered his voice as he leaned toward his uncle. "She is on our side when it comes to this. We are going to prove to both of them that this will never work in the long run. We can only do that if we let them see into each other's worlds. It's a good plan. It's going to work."

Oliver side-eyed him but stayed quiet. They ordered their hot chocolate and started making their way back to the family.

"It's a good plan," Oliver admitted. "But we need to have a backup in case we run out of time. While I figure out what that is, I need you to do whatever you can to help make planning this wedding a challenge. Tell her no one can do the flowers, call all the bakeries and tell them I'll pay them not to bake a wedding cake. Whatever it takes."

Jonah wasn't going to need to pay off bakeries. His grandmother would be backing out of this wedding in no time. Randall was sure to show his true colors.

They returned to the family just as the tree-lighting ceremony got underway. Jonah's phone vibrated with a text. It was Holly letting him know she was back with Randall. He sent a quick message with their general whereabouts so they could find each other.

"Clarissa," Randall called out when they were close.

Gran's head turned and her face lit up at the sight of him. They embraced and the entire family stood frozen in place as they bore witness to this public display of affection.

Jonah nodded a hello as Holly came up behind her great-uncle. She probably felt exactly like he did last night at the Roadrunner—outnumbered. Holly always came across as the toughest person in the room. It was strange to see her nervous. Vulnerability was something she probably avoided like the plague. The urge to protect her shocked him. Holly Hayward never needed protecting.

He shuffled past his cousin and her family to get next to Holly. "No trouble getting him here?"

"Nope. As soon as he heard she was hoping to see him and that I was willing to come along, he was all for it."

"Let the fun begin," Jonah whispered back.

The mayor took the stage and welcomed everyone to the festivities. She gave a similar speech every year. It always began with what a wonderful year it had been and how the town of Coyote was prospering. She talked of the joy of Christmas and the hopes for the new year. Finally, she led the crowd in a countdown before flipping the switch that turned on the tree lights.

Jonah glanced in Holly's direction. A sweet smile played on her lips. The twinkling lights reflected in her eyes. She tapped her foot to the Christmas carol that played over the loudspeakers. She was enjoying this.

"You're glad you came, aren't you?" he asked.

She quickly controlled her expression. "I'll be glad when our plan works."

Jonah's attention shifted to his grandmother and Randall. They were standing close and holding hands. It was...cute. This part of the evening wasn't helping with the plan.

"Who's ready to go ice-skating?" he asked, knowing his cousin's kids would cheerfully reply.

Randall's eyes went wide with surprise. Holly had not mentioned what else they'd be doing. "Maybe us older folk should go find a place to get warm," he suggested.

Gran was having none of that. "And miss skating in the square? It's one of my favorite things to do!"

Jonah felt giddy, knowing Randall was no skater. He could see Holly was equally pleased. He was falling right in their trap.

"Well, then I guess we're all going skating," the old man replied with a less than enthusiastic expression.

The family made their way to the skating rink on the other end of the square. Julia's family had all brought skates. The rest of them had to rent some.

"You love ice-skating? How often do you skate?" Randall asked Gran while they laced up their skates.

"I used to skate for fun when I was young. Competed in a few ice shows. Nothing too exciting. These days, I go out a few times each winter with the children."

Gran was being modest. She had actually been an amazing ice dancer. She had not only been in shows, she had won some major competitions.

"What about you, Randall? You much of a skater?" Jonah asked.

"We didn't have much money growing up and ice skates weren't something our mom and dad could afford. My brother and I used to play hockey on the frozen pond behind our house, but we did it in our boots with brooms instead of sticks and a frozen cow pie for a puck."

Holly burst out in laughter. "How have I never heard this story before? A cow pie? That's so gross, Uncle Randall."

"Hey, sometimes you gotta get creative to have a little fun," he said, clearly unashamed.

"I didn't realize you've never skated before," Gran said, sounding a bit alarmed. "I don't want you to go out there and break a hip. That would make it very hard to dance with you on our wedding day."

Randall chuckled and patted her on the knee. "I won't break anything, my dear. I was a rodeo cowboy, remember? I'm nearly indestructible."

Holly didn't look so sure, either. "Maybe she's right, Uncle Randall. Maybe you and I should watch while the Drakes take a few laps around the rink."

"Have you ever skated?" Jonah asked Holly, suddenly suspicious of her desire to stay off the ice as well.

"We went ice-skating on a field trip when we were in eighth grade, don't you remember?"

Jonah remembered a lot of things, but that particular memory hadn't stuck. "Can't say I remember that one."

"Well, we went to a real ice-skating rink and I skated."

"So, one time. You've skated one time."

"I bet I can still skate better than you," she replied indignantly.

Typical Holly, turning everything into a competition. "I have skated every winter since I moved to Coyote. I would be careful who you challenge to a skating race."

"Oh boy, your grandson does not know who he is messing with, does he?" Randall said to Gran.

Holly tightened the laces on her skates and double-knotted them. "I think you might be scared about getting beat by a woman who has only skated once."

How could he back down from that? "Let's go, Hayward."

She had no fear. She headed right for that rink without any hesitation, and then almost had both feet go right out from under her as soon as she stepped on the ice. Jonah caught her, holding her up until she regained her balance.

"I've got it," Holly asserted as she wiggled out of his grasp. Struggling to stay on her feet, she grabbed hold of the sidewall.

"I don't know about this. Maybe we shouldn't try to race. Let's just carefully make our way around the rink. No one needs to get hurt." Jonah could see her taking out a few people on her way down if she tried to go through with this.

"I'm not going to get hurt."

"Of course not. I just think it's a little too crowded out here for us to do anything that could lead to someone—anyone—getting hurt. I don't think we need to show off in front of all these people. You and I can come back and race when there are no little kids to get in our way." He was desperately trying to give her an out.

Holly tried to let go of the wall and almost slipped. Clinging to the wall for support, she attempted to save face. "Fine, if you're not sure you can make your way around the rink without hitting some innocent kid, I can wait to beat you another day."

Jonah sighed with relief. He held out his hand. "Care to join me for a slow glide to the other side?"

She was holding on for dear life. She bit down on her lower lip as she contemplated letting go.

"Come on, Holly. We can do it," Randall said, coming out on the ice. The old man wobbled but managed to stay up. "Could someone just push me so I don't have to lift my feet?"

Gran offered him her hand. "I'll pull you along. Once you get used to being on the ice, then you can try to move yourself."

Jonah looked back at Holly, still stuck to the wall like glue. "We need to keep up with them if we're going to make sure they're having a terrible time."

Holly took a deep breath and tested out letting go. She didn't fall, so she reached for Jonah's hand. She wobbled, but he steadied her. "I won't let you fall," he said.

Holly got a dazed look in her eye. Jonah interlocked their arms and made sure she was good. He slowly moved them across the ice. It didn't take them long to catch up to his grandmother and her terrified beau.

"You look a little nervous, Randall. This isn't even Gran's usual pace. How are you going to keep up with her if you can't even lift your feet?"

"He's doing a good job," Gran said in his defense. "I don't mind slowing down for him. Plus, I can still throw in some of my fancy moves." She lifted their arms and did a twirl.

Randall's fear seemed to melt away. She kept hold of his hand while she did some of her old dance moves. She was so graceful that she never once caused him to lose his balance.

"Holy cow, your grandmother is really good at skating," Holly said, showing a little more confidence on those thin blades. "Can you do that kind of stuff?"

Jonah shook his head. "No way. I didn't inherit her footwork skills. I go one direction and can manage to take wide turns without losing my balance. She's a trained professional. I'm recreation only."

Holly was smiling again, which was a good sign. "I hope when I'm in my eighties, I'm still good at the things I did when I was young."

"I mean, if nothing else, you should still be excellent at making sarcastic comments and bad jokes."

"Bad jokes?" Holly said with a huff. "I do not tell bad jokes. I am funny. I get tipped at work all the time for being so funny."

"Oh, let's be honest. You get tipped at

work because you're beautiful. You would probably get more tips if you cut back on the jokes and sarcasm."

Holly's cheeks went from pink to red. "Beautiful?"

Jonah didn't even realize what he'd said. He hadn't meant to say that. It was true, but he knew better than to compliment her about her looks. Women like Holly didn't want to be called pretty. She had always wanted to be recognized for what she could do, not how she looked. "You know what I mean. You're not unattractive. And the guys who go drinking at the Roadrunner definitely think you're pretty. Right?"

"The guys who drink at the Roadrunner think that any woman with two eyes, a nose and a mouth is pretty. I guess I fall in that category." She loosened her grip on his arm. "I do think they appreciate my sense of humor, though. And my excellent skills at mixing drinks."

"I'm sure you're one of the best," Jonah replied, smiling because he was right again. Holly hadn't changed much since high school.

Gran and Randall did two more loops before they decided to call it a night. Jonah hadn't been hoping for any major injuries, but that had gone almost too well. They were both still completely smitten.

"Ice-skating might not have been our best chance at ruining this relationship," Holly said as they continued around the rink. "I think Uncle Randall had fun."

"We still have time. There's no way he's going to have any fun at the gingerbread contest. Even I find it a bit boring. Gran, on the other hand, takes it very seriously. She scolds me every year for not trying harder or appreciating the works of art. You think Randall is going to be wowed by ginger-bread and gumdrops?"

"I am fairly certain that Randall has never been in a baking competition and the man hates the taste of gingerbread. We've always made our gingerbread men out of sugar cookie dough because of him."

Jonah could feel his brows pinch together. "Can you call them gingerbread men if they're made out of sugar cookie dough?"

"You're always so technical. Loosen up, Jonah. Call a sugar cookie man a ginger-bread man. It's okay. The gingerbread men of the world will not come after you with little gingerbread pitchforks if you let it slide."

Jonah snorted. "Tiny gingerbread pitchforks?" The image of gingerbread men with pitchforks chasing him around the house made him giggle.

Holly smirked. "I'm funny. I told you this."

She was funny. And beautiful. And a Hayward. He couldn't forget their entire reason for being together was to keep their families apart. She was not going to charm her way into his heart like Randall had done to Gran. That was never happening.

CHAPTER FOUR

"GRAN, WE HAVE to leave if you want to get there five minutes early," Jonah shouted up the stairs.

His mom made her way down. "She's fixing her hair. Ever since you told her that Randall was coming to the competition with Holly, she's been all aflutter."

Ever since the ice-skating backfired, Gran had been nothing but excited for the gingerbread event. Jonah was sure that Randall would not fare as well at the Coyote Social Club as he did at the tree lighting. His true colors were sure to shine through.

Randall had a reputation for being quite the ladies' man. He was also known as a love-'em-and-leave-'em type. There were going to be lots of ladies at this event. All of Gran's friends either judged or were entered. Plenty of fish for him to flirt with today. Hopefully, he would give in to old habits.

Gran came downstairs dressed in her favorite Christmas sweater. It was white with a row of gingerbread houses across the chest. She had little gingerbread men dangling from her ears and her fingernails were striped like candy canes.

"You look nice, Gran."

"Oh, stop," she said, digging through her purse for something. She pulled out a tube of lipstick.

Jonah and his mom exchanged looks. Jonah had to press his lips together to hold in a chuckle. Gran was always well put together, but lipstick was usually reserved for fancy occasions. The gingerbread competition was not usually a lipstick-worthy event.

There was a knock at the door and Carter Hanes let himself in. Carter helped run the ranch. "I know you all are heading out, but Annabelle is getting a little fussy and I wondered if you wanted to check on her before you left."

Annabelle was a pregnant mare. She was Gran's favorite horse and this was her first pregnancy.

"Yeah, I can come take a look." Jonah winked at his grandmother. "You just earned yourself a couple more minutes to make yourself gorgeous."

She scowled at him. "Don't tease an old woman. Go make sure my horse is all right."

Jonah followed Carter to the horse barn. Annabelle snorted as soon as he approached her stall.

"Brought her in because she was making some ornery noises and walking around like she was anxious," Carter said.

"No flirty nickering from you today? Are you snorting at me because you're mad you got brought inside or because something's bothering you? Huh, sweet girl?" Jonah gave her a little scratch on the neck as her tail swished. He checked her out and assessed nothing was out of the ordinary for a mare this close to giving birth. "We're getting there, Annabelle. You've got a couple more uncomfortable weeks. I'm sorry about that."

"Will she be fine outside or should I keep her in her stall?"

"She's going to be walking around and grumbling. Probably better to let her do it in the field than making her feel confined in here. She's uncomfortable, but there's not much I can do about that right now. It's the joy of motherhood."

"My mama always said it's a good thing women have the babies because if the good Lord had asked men to do that, we'd be extinct," Carter joked.

Jonah nodded. "That is probably true." He laughed as he put Annabelle's harness on so he could lead her back outside.

"I don't mean to pry, but there is one heck of a rumor going around town that Mrs. Drake is engaged to Randall Hayward. Word is that he proposed to her a couple nights ago. That can't possibly be true, can it?"

Carter had been working for the family for quite some time. He knew of the rift between the two families. Jonah could only imagine the gossip that had been traveling across town over the last few days.

"I know it doesn't seem possible, but it is true. She accepted his proposal the other night. We're all a little stunned and still trying to wrap our heads around it."

"Your grandfather has got to be rolling in his grave. Those two men did not like one another."

Jonah scratched the back of his neck. He was well aware of how devastated his grandfather would be if he knew what was happening in his absence. Hopefully, Jonah and Holly would put an end to this silly relationship and there would be no need for his grandfather to be upset up there in heaven.

"It's a strange situation for sure. I'd appreciate your discretion when talking to others around town. Who knows what is really going to come of this and we'd like to keep things private for now."

Carter tipped his hat. "You got it, Mr. Drake. I'm not one for gossip. Just wanted to make sure people weren't making up stories about the missus. She's always been good to me and I'd hate for anyone to be spreading mistruths about her."

"That's very kind of you, Carter." Hopefully no one would be talking about Gran soon enough. It was time to go to the gingerbread competition and get this wedding canceled as soon as possible.

Jonah had been raised that on time meant five minutes early. Being on time was late and being late was simply unacceptable. Today, given Gran's need for extra primping and Annabelle's protest about being ten months pregnant, they were late. No one seemed to notice except Penelope Trenton.

Mrs. Trenton greeted them as if they had waltzed in midcontest. "Clarissa! You made it. We thought we were going to have to replace you. Genevieve was just about to start making calls."

"Well, my dear. I'd hope the first call would have been to me so I could have assured you we were on our way. We have a pregnant mare and she needed Jonah's help this morning. Since he was my ride, I couldn't help our tardiness."

Jonah had no problem taking the blame, but she was lucky that Carter had asked for the checkup when he did. He would have loved to hear what kind of excuse she would have given if he hadn't been one of the reasons they didn't leave earlier.

"I don't know how she's going to be an impartial judge this year when she's clearly trying very hard to keep Mr. Hayward interested," his mom said as they took their jackets over to the coat check.

"I have a feeling that Mr. Hayward isn't going to make a gingerbread house that will be a close contender for grand champion. Holly said he hates gingerbread and I am assuming that means he hasn't made a lot of gingerbread houses in his lifetime."

"Your grandmother will be terribly bothered if he doesn't like gingerbread. She was just asking me if I thought it would be a sweet gesture to bake him some cookies."

"I think we won't have to worry about her making any kind gestures soon enough. Let's hope today is her first glimpse into the real Randall Hayward."

"Did someone say my name?"

Jonah turned around to find Randall and Holly right behind him. It appeared they had brought along two little ones as well. Holly had on one of the most heinous ugly Christmas sweaters he'd ever seen. It had a gingerbread man with one leg missing. In bold letters it read, BITE ME. It had to be wrong that he loved it so much.

"You're sure we don't have to be members of the club to join in the holiday fun today?" Holly asked, once again looking a little out of place.

He immediately felt the need to reassure

her. "Everyone is welcome. I signed you up, remember?"

"We brought along two extra helpers. My niece and nephew are here to see to it that Uncle Randall wins. He convinced them he needed their help. If that's not allowed, we totally understand and I can call my sister and have her pick them up pronto."

Clearly, she had been foiled in her plans to get Randall here alone so he could fail miserably. There was no way Jonah could send two little kids home after they had been told they could make a gingerbread house. Jonah's mom helped Randall get the kids out of their jackets.

"They're like what…five years old?"

"Gia is five, Patrick is four. They are very messy. Maybe that's a good thing?" she asked, lowering her voice so only Jonah could hear.

"Will they at some point infuriate him by chance?"

"He has never spent more than a few minutes alone with them." A broad smile broke out across her face. "This actually could be a disaster."

They slyly high-fived. Jonah noticed that

Randall took a peek into the room to the left where there was a fully stocked bar and fancy velvet couches and wingback chairs for the members to sit and enjoy a cocktail. If that man had a choice, he would definitely choose to spend the day in there.

Unfortunately for him, he was headed the other direction. To the right was the club's main room where the competition was going to take place. It was filled mostly with women somewhere between his mother's and his grandmother's ages, a few families and absolutely no single men except for Jonah. Randall was going to have many ladies to resist wooing.

"Randall, you made it." Gran had a clipboard in hand and her voice was an octave higher than usual.

They embraced and Randall gave her a kiss on the cheek. "Wouldn't miss it, my dear. May I just say, you look absolutely beautiful this morning."

"Oh, please. I practically rolled out of bed like this."

"Another reason I can't wait to wake up each day with you by my side." Randall gently took her hand and kissed the top of it.

Gran sighed like something straight out of a regency-era romance movie.

Jonah and his mom once again exchanged looks and tried not to laugh. Who was this woman and what had she done with his grandmother?

UNCLE RANDALL WAS the king of compliments. He'd been making the women of Coyote and the surrounding areas swoon for decades. Clarissa Drake was no exception. She had fallen for his charm hook, line and sinker.

This meant Holly was going to have to expose this rose's thorns. She loved her great-uncle, but the man was one giant flirt and hadn't been in a committed relationship for as long as she had been alive. There was no way this tiger just changed his stripes.

"I see you brought along some helpers."

Randall gathered the little ones in front of him and placed a hand on each one's shoulder. "These are my grandniece's children, Gia and Parker."

"Patrick," Holly corrected him.

"Patrick. That's what I said. Gia and Patrick."

Holly had to admit, she was looking forward to this. They might be done with all this Christmas wedding talk by lunchtime.

"Well, let's get you all situated. Will all four of you be working on one house?" Clarissa asked as she led them into the main room.

Holly had never been inside the social club before. It was for the Coyote elite. She had friends who had worked there, but no one she hung out with was a member. The main room was decorated to the extreme for the holidays. Garland covered in glittery ornaments was strung up everywhere. Bouquets of poinsettias in a variety of colors were scattered all around the room. There were three huge Christmas trees in one corner. This year's theme was snow so they were covered in snowflake ornaments, silver ribbon and a million lights. An inflatable snowman stood in front of a winter wonderland backdrop for a photo op in the other corner.

"I want to win," Holly replied. "To do that, I have to work alone."

"Of course," Jonah said with a sigh.

"Of course?" It annoyed her that he always had a comment. Almost as much as it bothered her that he had shown up here in his forest green button-down and dark jeans, looking like he could break someone's heart. He also hadn't shaved this morning, so his five-o'clock shadow was in full effect and causing her to have unwanted thoughts of standing close enough to touch his face.

"Of course you want to win. And of course you want to work alone. You're very predictable."

"Isn't that the whole point of entering a contest? To win?"

The corners of his mouth curled up ever so slightly. "Some people come to simply enjoy their time with their family and friends."

"Oh, I get it. You've never won, have you?"

The space between his eyebrows creased and he blew a dismissive breath. "I could win if I wanted to, but I tend to let my mother choose the design of our house."

His mom gasped. "Are you saying I'm the reason we never win?"

"No." His backpedaling began. "I mean you do it for fun, not to compete against the people here who take it so seriously."

"Maybe we shouldn't work together this year and you can be as serious as you want." She made it sound like she was giving him a choice, but she was also clearly letting him know he was on his own from now on.

"Mom…" he tried, but she wouldn't have it.

"Oh, someone is in trouble," Randall said with a chuckle. Holly couldn't help but giggle herself.

Jonah was solely focused on Holly when he said, "Well, now you're going to lose."

"Looks like Jonah and I will need our own houses to decorate, Mrs. Drake," she said to Clarissa without breaking eye contact with Jonah. How hard could it be to win this thing?

Four rows of five rectangle banquet tables each were lined up and covered in snowflake-patterned plastic tablecloths. Each table had one or two sets of premade gingerbread house pieces laid out.

Clarissa explained the setup. "Families working as a group are at the tables here on this side of the room where there's one house per table. Individuals building their houses solo are in the front row where there are two houses per table. Do you two think you can manage sitting at the same table?"

"We can handle it, Gran," Jonah answered for them.

Holly decided she should sit by him to make sure he didn't cheat or get help from anyone else.

Once everyone had been checked in and seated, the rules of the contest were explained by the judges. Everyone had one hour to glue their houses together with the icing provided and decorate it with the goodies supplied on the round tables up front. They were loaded with every kind of candy one could imagine. There were the usual—gumdrops, candy-coated chocolates, peppermints and mini marshmallows—but there were also things like licorice strings, chocolate nonpareils, those sweet-and-sour candies and spearmint jellies.

Holly didn't do a lot of cooking or baking, but she did love to watch baking shows and people decorate desserts on social media. She had observed enough to know what she needed to do to create a showstopper.

"You're going to regret challenging me to a gingerbread duel," Jonah warned her as they announced everyone could begin. "Left to my own devices, I may not only win, but make the house they'll talk about for years to come."

"I'm sure they'll be talking about it. About how it struggled to even stand up," Holly replied with a smirk as the two walls Jonah had tried to connect with icing slipped apart and fell flat. This would be too easy.

Holly kept an eye on Randall and the children, who were seated behind them and one table over. They also seemed to be struggling. Both kids wanted to be the one who squeezed out the icing and were currently fighting for the pastry bag. Icing was squirting out everywhere except on the gingerbread. Randall looked nauseous. He hated gingerbread and its scent hung heavy in the room.

"Maybe you should be in charge of the icing," a woman sitting on the other side of Randall suggested. "Let the little ones be in charge of the candy. They love that part."

"That sounds like an excellent idea. Kids, go up there and pick out some candy. I'll get the house put together and you can decorate it."

Holly quickly recognized she was Mrs. Hille, a former Coyote Elementary School teacher. She was recently widowed and seemingly here by herself. Mrs. Hille continued to converse with Randall about all things gingerbread. She laughed at his cookie puns and he complimented her icing work.

It was all going splendidly. Holly checked to make sure Clarissa had noticed how well the two of them were getting along and there was no doubt she had. Clarissa's gaze was locked on Randall and her lips were pressed into a thin line.

Holly happily focused on her masterpiece as the plan was working, and Jonah had finally figured out how to get his walls to stand up.

"Mr. Hayward, I believe these two belong to you," Mrs. Trenton said gruffly a few minutes later. She had Gia and Patrick by the arms. "They've been standing up at the candy table, unsupervised I might add, shoveling candy into their mouths for the last five minutes. This is not an all-you-can-eat candy buffet, Mr. Hayward. Children need to stay with the adult in charge of them."

"I told you two to pick out some candy for the house, not your bellies," Randall scolded them.

"Holly and I can supervise them up there to get some candy," Jonah offered. "Come on, you rascals."

That was an excellent plan since the kids would distract Randall from his new friend. "Mrs. Trenton almost ruined everything. He's paying Mrs. Hille way more attention than your grandmother likes."

"I noticed that. Not to mention she'll be disappointed in the way he handled the children once Mrs. Trenton tells her all about how they were ransacking the candy table." His grin was as wide as hers was. Their plan was working perfectly.

"You guys have to pick out candy you want to put on your house. Take one of these bowls and put the candy in there to bring back to the table. No more candy in your mouth," Holly reminded her niece and nephew.

Jonah held Patrick's hand as they perused their options. He crouched down to hear what the little guy was saying about needing some marshmallows and helped him spoon some into his bowl.

As if his unshaven face wasn't enough to distract her from the task at hand, now he had to pull being sweet to a little kid as well. She chalked up these feelings to the fact that she always fell for the wrong kinds of guys. She had a real talent for finding the ones who were least suitable to be her partner in life. Jonah Drake would be no exception. Not only were they complete opposites, Jonah was a Drake. He would always be Mr. Wrong.

Gia tugged on Holly's sleeve. The little girl looked absolutely green. "My belly hurts."

Before Holly could state the obvious about the dangers of eating too much candy, the kindergartener threw up on the floor and all over Holly's boots.

"I feel better now," Gia announced.

Holly stood frozen in horror. Jonah swooped in and took Gia by the hand. "Whoa, that's a lot of half-eaten candy. Wow! I don't think I've ever seen anything like that before. I've got the kids, why don't you get yourself cleaned up?"

As the ladies in charge of this event came running to handle the biohazard at Holly's feet, she made a quick exit to the bathroom. She grabbed a wad of paper towels and wiped the sugary puke off her boots.

"What a mess out there. I don't think I've ever seen so much stuff come out of such a little body before." Holly looked up to find Janet Williams hovering over her. Janet and Holly had been in the same graduating class but were never friends. "Those are Maisy's kids, right?"

"They are." Holly went back to scrubbing her boots.

"I thought so. I mean, I knew they weren't yours. Or Jonah's. Are you and Jonah here together? I noticed you came in together and he was helping you with the kids. I thought you and the Drakes didn't like each other."

Nosy people were Holly's least favorite kind of people. "Jonah and I did not come together. I came with my family and he came with his."

"So you two aren't dating or anything like that?"

Holly barked out a laugh. Was she serious? "We are not dating."

Janet seemed relieved and walked over to the mirror to check her reflection. She smoothed her hair down and reapplied some lipstick. Holly tossed the paper towel in the garbage. She could see what was going on here.

Janet kept talking as she gussied herself up. "I can't believe that man is still single. He's got to be the most eligible bachelor in town."

If eye-rolling was a sport, Holly would have won a gold medal. "I don't know about that."

Janet dabbed the corner of her mouth with her pinkie finger. "Okay, maybe he's just behind your uncle now that he won the lottery."

That was what Holly was hoping. The more popular Randall was, the more Clarissa would second-guess agreeing to marry him. "He was pretty popular with the widows in this town before that. Who knows what it will be like now."

"I thought I heard he proposed to Jonah's grandmother. Didn't he take himself off the market?"

Holly washed her hands at the sink next

to her. "I guess, but anything could happen to change that."

"Oh boy. The Drakes win again."

"Excuse me?" Holly shook her hands before grabbing another paper towel.

"Your family finally strikes it rich and the one with the money immediately decides to tie himself to a Drake. Isn't that your family's worst nightmare?"

Holly didn't appreciate that this engagement made it look as if the Drakes were besting them. "We're doing just fine, thank you. Randall hasn't tied himself to anything yet."

"I guess they could always sign a serious prenup, right?"

No one in the Hayward family had ever needed such a thing. Randall would be the first, and that was necessary if he did end up going through with this marriage.

Janet dropped her lipstick back in her purse. "Since it sounds like Randall's spoken for at the moment at least, that puts Jonah back on the top of the most eligible list. I, for one, would be happy to take him off of there."

Holly should have told her to go for it because it shouldn't have bothered her one bit that Janet wanted to date Jonah or that Jonah might want to date Janet. Only it did. She tried to brush it off. These feelings were surely related to the fact that she didn't want him distracted from helping her stop the wedding. It couldn't possibly be because of anything else.

CHAPTER FIVE

THINGS WERE NOT going the way they were supposed to be going. Since Holly had gone to clean up, Randall was making a comeback. He had stopped talking to Mrs. Hille and was completely focused on his gingerbread house. He had the kids sorting the candy by color and they were perfect angels at the moment.

Jonah glanced in the direction of the bathrooms, hoping Holly would return to stir the pot somehow. She was nowhere to be seen. He wondered if he should check on her. What happened to her was pretty disgusting, after all.

"Well, hello there, Dr. Drake." Janet Williams suddenly appeared in front of him.

"Hi, Janet." He gave her a quick smile before returning his gaze to the bathrooms.

"I noticed you were staring at me when

I came out of the ladies' room. Thought I'd better come over and see how you're doing."

That got his attention. "You were just in the bathroom? Did you see Holly Hayward in there?"

Janet wore a confused expression. "Holly? Yeah, she's in there."

"Is everything okay? Does she need help? Should I have someone check on her?"

"She's fine. She should be out in a second. You should have seen her face when I asked her if you guys were here together. She looked like she was about to throw up. That woman sure likes to hold a grudge, doesn't she?"

Jonah felt that like a punch to the stomach. Hadn't they been getting along for the most part? Why did she always have to act like they were bitter enemies? He couldn't think of anything that he had personally done to make her hold a grudge.

"Your gingerbread house is looking good. I can't believe you're doing this all by yourself. My mom and nana are doing most of the work on ours. I'll help when it's time to add the candy bling. That's my favorite part," Janet continued.

Holly had reentered the room. She moved with purpose, her eyes locked on Jonah. She seemed flustered. Was she mad at him?

Janet was still talking. "I'd love to help you if you need it. I'm telling you, I'm good at the candy part."

"Wow, you guys are doing such a good job," Holly said to Randall and her niece and nephew in quite the sugary tone. The look she shot Jonah, though, showed she was displeased.

He tried his best to nonverbally communicate that he was at a loss for how to stir the pot.

"Jonah?" Janet said, trying to get his attention.

He didn't know what she wanted from him, but he had work to do. "Good luck on your gingerbread," he said to Janet before sliding over to Holly's workspace. He lowered his voice as he leaned in close to Holly. "He's like a man on a mission. Things were going so well and then he just started putting the house together like some kind of pro."

"We need to lure some other single grannies over here," Holly whispered. "Hopefully he'll pay them better attention than you showed Janet."

"Janet?"

"She left the bathroom determined to catch your eye, but man, she didn't catch anything but a chill from your cold shoulder."

"What?" Jonah glanced back at where Janet had been standing. Holly laughed, mumbling something about most eligible. They didn't have time for him to sort all that out. His grandmother was walking around and every time she looked Randall's way, she smiled. She was pleased with whatever he was doing.

"Marjorie Ratcliffe," Holly whispered as she went back to work on her own gingerbread house. "They used to date. I'll get her over here."

Holly finished securing all of her gingerbread walls and went up to the candy table, which was close to where Marjorie was talking to a friend. Jonah watched as Holly weaseled her way into their conversation. They were obviously talking about the unfortunate throw-up incident as Holly pointed to her boots and laughed.

She had an endearing laugh even when she was putting on an act. He liked the way the apples of her cheeks became more pronounced and her eyes crinkled at the corners. She could be quite charming when she was in a good mood.

Marjorie followed her back to their row of tables and greeted Randall with a kiss on the cheek. Jonah checked to see if his gran was watching, and she was. He gave Holly a thumbs-up.

"Now all I have to do is win this competition," Holly said, squirting some icing on a peppermint candy.

Jonah shook his head. Holly always had to win. He had to at least give her a run for her money. He stole a gumdrop from her bowl of candy.

"Hey! Get your own, buddy." She tried to sound mad, but her smile gave her away.

"I will and my house is going to be better than yours."

"Good luck," she said, getting back to her house decorating.

He wasn't afraid of a little challenge. He gathered up his own bowl of candy. His advantage would be that his house was going to have a theme. He was going to make his house a barn and stick to only red and white candies. He was also going to make some animals out of marshmallows.

Holly's was a mishmash of all the colors under the rainbow. She put a row of gumdrops down the center of her roof and used multicolored candy-coated chocolates like Christmas lights along her roofline. She was impressive.

"What is that? A weird snowman?" she asked as he manipulated some marshmallows.

"It's a dog." He held it up and pinched its nose. "It looks like a dog, doesn't it?"

Holly's eyebrows lifted. "Sure."

"Oh, come on." Jonah tried to fix its tail and make it a little longer.

There was that laugh again as she shook her head. "I'm not going to humor you and tell you it looks like a dog when it doesn't. I'm sorry."

"I think I know a dog when I see one. I am a veterinarian."

"And I would have thought a man as familiar with animal anatomy as you would be a bit more capable of creating something that at least resembled a dog."

He wasn't going to be intimidated by her trash talk. "You'll see when it's finished. Mine is going to be a showstopper."

Mrs. Trenton called out that there were only ten minutes left. Jonah could see that Holly's house was coming together better than his. He used the icing to make some snow piles around his barn and animals, then quickly pulled apart some licorice strings to line the walkway he had made earlier. He wiped his brow when Mrs. Trenton called time.

Holly cheated and continued adding some green spearmint jellies beside her front door that looked like trees.

"She called time. Put the candy down or I'm reporting you to my grandmother," he warned.

"I am owed some extra minutes since I had to take a time-out to clean puke off my boots."

"Sorry, no time-outs. That's what you get for bringing your sister's kids. That's on you."

In retaliation, she knocked over his marshmallow horse. "Uh-oh, your dog fell over."

"That's not my dog. That's my horse."

"That was a horse?" she said with a snorting laugh.

"Your trees were added after time was called." Jonah grabbed one of her spearmint trees and popped it in his mouth.

"Hey!" She reached for one of his peppermint-stick fence posts, but he blocked her attempted sabotage.

His mother intervened. "Children, let's make sure we're setting a good example for all the smaller children here."

Holly and Jonah both returned to their respective side of the table and clasped their hands behind their backs. Holly tried to fight a smile by biting her lip. Jonah didn't hold back his grin as he finished chewing the candy in his mouth.

Even if he didn't win, this year's gingerbread competition was better than all the rest combined.

HOLLY TOOK ANOTHER look at Jonah's house and knew she had won. He could eat all her trees and she would still beat his red-and-white monstrosity.

"Wow, your house looks nice, Auntie Holly," Gia said.

"Thanks, sweetie. I think it does, too. Better than Mr. Drake's, right?"

"Really?" Jonah questioned with a nudge. He tried to sway Gia to disagree. "Mine is a barn with all these animals. Isn't that neat?"

"Where are the animals?" Gia asked with a furrowed brow.

Holly could not love her niece more. His animals looked like squished piles of marshmallows. He should probably just tell the judges they were snow piles.

"The judges will now walk around and score each house on creativity, construction and overall presentation. When we're finished, please enjoy some refreshments while we compile the scores."

"Our house has Santa going down the chimney," Gia announced.

Holly and Jonah had been so focused on their own houses they had stopped paying attention to how Randall and the kids were doing. She had hoped that Marjorie had distracted him while ruffling Clarissa's feathers at the same time.

They turned around to find Uncle Randall had managed to create the most amazing gingerbread house Holly had ever seen. He had somehow put together perfectly square walls with invisible seams. There was no icing oozing from the edges like on hers. The roof was securely attached and covered in chocolate discs that were layered like shingles. He had fashioned a chimney out of brick-shaped hard candies and made it look like Santa had gone down it headfirst by turning black licorice into boots and sticking them out the top.

Holly went over there for a closer look. Shocked, all she could ask was, "How?"

"This was actually kind of fun," Randall said. "Reminded me of when your grandpa and I used to play with the scraps left over from our daddy's projects. We used to pretend we were building skyscrapers in the big city."

After getting cheated by the Drake family, Holly's great-grandfather had a bunch of odd jobs. He had worked on ranches, did some construction, even had a job selling vacuums at one time. He had loved working with his hands the most, even helped build some of the old barns in Coyote.

Jonah came up beside her. "How did you make everything so clean-looking? Where is the icing that holds it all together?"

"It's all on the inside. Haven't you ever caulked a shower before? I just ran a bead of icing where the two walls meet and smoothed it out with my finger. Worked pretty good, huh?"

It had worked too well. He was going to get bonus points for his construction skills.

"Did Marjorie help you decorate?" Holly asked. How else could he have made it look so good?

"No, but thanks for bringing her over. She helped keep the kids entertained so I could stay focused. She also gave me a couple good ideas that she thought would impress the judges." He winked. "Especially Clarissa."

Holly couldn't look at Jonah. He had to be thinking all this was her fault. It had been her idea to bring Marjorie over after all.

"I think my gran is going to love it," Jonah said. "You did a great job, Randall."

The judges made their way around the room. Holly began to stress-eat her leftover candy until they reached her table. They judged Holly's first. They liked her creativity and her use of color. They noted her excellent piping skills and the swirly details she piped around the windows. They moved on to Jonah, who immediately tried to explain his barn concept. They liked his red-and-white design but didn't seem impressed with the marshmallow creatures he was trying to pass off as animals. The judges were kind but not as effusive with their compliments as they were with Holly.

"They definitely gave you more points than they gave me. Even though you were missing one of your trees," Jonah said, pulling the other tree off her board and popping it in his mouth. "Your trees that were added after time was called."

"Aw, don't be a sore loser."

"Like you were with the ice-skating competition?"

"I did not lose the skating competition. We decided together to do it another time."

"That's right. I'm sure had we had an

open rink, you would have wiped the floor with me."

Holly couldn't lie. "The only thing that was about to be wiped was me. I would have wiped out for sure."

"I guess we're tied, then. One to one." He pulled one of the gumdrops off her roof and ate it. "Your house tastes better than mine, too."

He was so darn...cute. The fact that the word *cute* ran through her mind made Holly want to cringe. Working together for a common goal was messing with her head. They were still on opposite teams.

The judges finally made their way to Randall's table. Clarissa beamed with pride. Her fiancé had outdone himself. Holly's mission was a complete failure. It was embarrassing that she had been so confident when she walked in. The judges asked Randall a few questions and he was his usual charming self, making the three ladies giggle.

Holly would have felt better about her impending win versus Jonah if things between Randall and Clarissa had gone worse. Randall, Gia and Patrick went to check out the refreshments they were offering once the judges left their table.

"Randall's going to win," Jonah bemoaned.

"He totally is." Holly glanced around the room at the other houses. None of them compared to her great-uncle's. "How did he manage it? He was supposed to hate this. He was supposed to flirt because decorating this house was going to be too much for him."

"Maybe Gran's Christmas activities aren't enough to scare him away. He wants to impress her, so he tried his best at ice-skating and gingerbread house decorating. Gran will have a harder time assimilating to his likes. I don't think all hope is lost."

"There you go, throwing your big words around." Holly had always been a bit intimidated by Jonah's intelligence. She'd envied his smarts as well as his endless curiosity when they were in school.

"Come on, what big word did I use?"

"Assimilating?"

"Don't act like you don't know what I'm saying. You love to make me feel like some kind of weirdo."

"I do not. Being smart doesn't make you

weird, but it does make me think you like making me feel dumb."

Jonah's jaw ticked. "You think I say things to make you feel dumb? I would never intentionally do that, Holly. You have to believe me."

She shrugged a shoulder, her gaze fixed on the floor between them. "You've been doing it since we were kids."

"Seriously? You have always made me more self-conscious than I could ever make you. You, with all your sarcasm, used to get everyone to laugh at me."

That wasn't the way she remembered it at all. "What are you talking about? I used to make some smart-aleck comments to deflect from the fact that I usually had no idea what you were talking about and everyone knew it. If they were laughing at anyone, it was me."

"I can't believe that's what you think happened." Jonah scratched the back of his head.

He seemed so sure of himself, but there was no way that wasn't exactly what happened. Maybe he hadn't done it on purpose like she had assumed, but the other people they grew up with definitely were laughing at her. Everyone loved Jonah.

"You don't remember that you were Mr. Popularity? You had everyone in this town bowing at your feet the minute you moved into town."

Jonah's mouth hung open for a moment. "Did we go to the same school?"

"I know we went to the same school because I had to listen to all those people go on and on about you. Were you really that oblivious? Mandy Geller used to write Mandy Drake in her notebook when we were all in biology class together and Quinn Miller used to plan how she would walk to classes based on where you were during the day. I used to have to listen to her talk about it at lunch with Anna Gregory. And nothing has changed in all these years. Janet Williams called you Coyote's most eligible bachelor today. It never ends. The amazing Jonah Drake. You can never do any wrong."

"Mandy Geller used to have a crush on me?"

Clearly oblivious. "Who didn't have a crush on you? Except for me, of course," she added for clarity. She didn't want him to

think she had ever been interested in someone with the last name Drake.

"Of course not. You made it crystal clear
that you did not like me the moment you
met me. You basically beat me up on my
first day."

Holly gasped. "What alternative universe
do you live in? I did not beat you up."

"You sure did. You kicked me and tried
to put bubble gum on my chair."

"I have no recollection of doing any such
things," she said, holding up a hand like she
was swearing in before a judge.

Jonah could have acted more resentful,
but he simply smirked. "Just because you
don't recollect, doesn't mean it didn't happen."

How could two people remember the
same things so differently? Holly wanted
to be sure they remembered the present the
same way. "I hope you don't forget in fif-
teen years that I beat you in this gingerbread
contest and that you were the one who tried
to sabotage me, not the other way around."

"You haven't won yet. I could pull a huge
upset thanks to my snow steed." He waved
a hand over his "horse."

Holly tsked. "Snow steed? That's a good one."

"It looks like a snow blob, doesn't it?"

She could only laugh. A snow blob was exactly what it was. What they all were.

"You know what these are good for?" he asked, pulling apart his marshmallow creatures. He threw one of the mini marshmallows at Holly, hitting her right on the forehead. "Snowball fight."

"Oh, bring it." Holly stood up and snatched what was maybe the dog. She quickly put some distance between them as he pelted her with his sticky snowballs.

She ducked and then began her own attack. She hit him twice in the chest and then one soared over his head and landed right in Mrs. Hille's hair. She thankfully didn't notice. Jonah's glee was written all over his face. He got out of his chair and grabbed Holly's hand, pulling her toward the other side of the room.

"We're going to get thrown out of here if we aren't careful. Do you want something to eat or should we get a picture with the snowman?"

Holly couldn't stop staring at their hands.

His hand was warm and soft. She liked the way hers felt in his. That was dangerous. She pulled it away.

"I'm going to check on Randall and the kids. I don't need Patrick to follow in his sister's footsteps. I've had enough throw up for one day." She made her escape, leaving him standing on the edge of the room wondering what her problem was.

He was her problem. She liked him. She liked him more than she should and that was not the purpose of this alliance. They were working together for one reason and one reason only—to keep their families from having anything to do with one another. Haywards and Drakes would never get along. History had proved that time and time again. Holly wished Jonah didn't make it so difficult to remember.

CHAPTER SIX

"THIS IS THE last one," Glenn Graves announced as they led one more calf into the squeeze chute for its vaccine.

Glenn owned one of the biggest dairy farms near Coyote. Jonah had spent the morning vaccinating the calves Glenn was getting ready to wean.

The last one was usually the one who gave Jonah the most trouble, but not today. This particular calf walked right in after the one before it exited.

"That was too easy." Jonah administered the pre-weaning vaccines. "Too bad they aren't all this way."

"We've been listening to you. I used to think they were afraid to go in because they remembered what happened to them when they were in the chute the last time, but you were very clear that they don't remember bad things, they remember bad handling. We've been working on that."

Jonah was happy to hear his advice was heeded and proved to be effective. "You made my job easier today and I appreciate that."

They finished and released the calf from the chute. Jonah secured his equipment and took off his gloves.

"I saw you at the social club the other day, Dr. Drake." Kendra Graves, Glenn's wife, had come outside to see how things were going. "You looked like you were having a good time."

This year's gingerbread contest would go down in history as one of his favorites. Even though it ended a bit strange and the ultimate mission had been a complete failure. His gran hadn't stopped talking about Randall's gingerbread house decorating skills since.

"It's always a good time. My grandmother loves judging all the houses."

"I noticed you and Holly Hayward were hitting it off. That's an interesting turn of events. Almost as interesting as Randall

Hayward and your grandmother's sudden engagement."

Small-town gossip was impossible to avoid. Jonah did his best to deflect and move on. "Christmas in Coyote is always interesting. Be sure to let me know if you notice anything off with the calves we vaccinated today. I can come back out if you need me."

"We will. Thank you, Dr. Drake," Glenn replied, offering him a handshake.

His wife wasn't finished digging for dirt. "I heard that your grandmother is planning a Christmas wedding. That's awfully fast. If they were younger, I'd wonder if it was a shotgun wedding."

Jonah didn't want to think about his grandmother making babies with Randall or anyone for that matter. "It's good we don't have to worry about that. I hope you both have a wonderful Christmas if I don't see you before then."

Kendra sighed, defeated in her attempts to get something out of him. "Merry Christmas to you as well," Glenn said.

Jonah loaded up his truck and headed back to the office to enter the vaccination records into his computer. He wondered if

Holly was getting as many questions about the upcoming nuptials as he was. Were people asking her about her relationship with him, too? Not that they had a relationship. They were simply working together to break up this wedding. Nothing more.

Not that he hadn't thought about more. Holly was fun to be around. She knew how to play, which wasn't true of all women their age. She also wasn't afraid to speak her mind; he always knew where she stood. He had dated some women in the past who were afraid to tell him what they were really thinking because they wanted him to like them. Didn't they know he wouldn't know if he liked them if he didn't know what was really going on in their heads? Holly didn't care if he liked her. In fact, she seemed more worried that he might like her than anything else.

It was Wednesday and they had only communicated via text as they made their plans to attend the Reindeer Rodeo on Thursday's opening night. Gran had seemed less than enthusiastic when she informed him that Randall had invited them to go. He thought she might try to get out of it by saying she was too busy planning this wedding, but she hadn't tried to bail yet.

Jonah drove back to his office. When he turned on Coyote Drive, he spotted Holly, her sister, Gia and Patrick coming out of the diner. The way his heart skipped a beat didn't go unnoticed.

He parked outside his clinic just as they were walking by. The sisters stopped conversing as soon as Holly made eye contact with him.

"Good morning," he said, trying to act like the last time they had seen each other hadn't ended so awkwardly. That she hadn't been repulsed by his touch and run away. That she hadn't left as soon as Randall was announced the winner of the overall contest without so much as a goodbye.

"Just rolling into work at ten thirty like a boss," Holly quipped.

"Rolling back into the office after spending the morning out at the Graves Dairy Farm vaccinating a bunch of calves. I don't spend much of my day here at the clinic. You're lucky we happened to bump into each other."

"She has no right to comment on anyone's starting time," Maisy said, coming to Jonah's defense much to her sister's dismay. "She gets out of bed after ten on the regular. Must be nice, right?"

"I guess I'm lucky we happened to bump into one another. You're usually brushing your teeth about this time on a regular day. You do brush your teeth, don't you?" he teased.

That got her to crack a smile. "I would have moved on to doing my hair by this time. As you can see—" she reached up and tapped the sloppy bun on top of her head "—getting up early to meet my sister for breakfast meant something had to give."

She was actually adorable in spite of her hasty morning routine. "I hope you can get yourself together tomorrow before the rodeo. I don't know if I can be seen with someone who doesn't take personal hygiene seriously."

"You two are going to the rodeo tomorrow? Together?" Maisy seemed surprised.

"I'm going with Randall. Jonah must be going with his grandmother, and Randall invited Clarissa to come with us, so I guess, yes, Jonah is coming with me and Randall. Not just me."

Maisy's face scrunched up in confusion. "Thanks for clarifying. That was…interesting."

What was interesting was that Maisy didn't appear to know about the plan. Wasn't the whole Hayward family in on this? Didn't she want the wedding stopped as much as everyone else?

"It should be a great time," Jonah said. "I haven't been to a rodeo in a few years. My dad loved to go with me. I'm looking forward to it."

Holly seemed anxious to find her way out of this conversation. "Well, I promise to look like this so you don't want to sit next to me. We should probably get the kids in the car. Bye, Jonah."

Maisy's expression somehow made her look more confused. "Bye, Jonah. It was good to see you."

"Bye, Mr. Drake," Gia said brightly. Patrick waved but stayed quiet.

There were no "I hate the Drakes" vibes coming off Maisy, which was refreshing.

Maybe not everyone surrounding Holly viewed him as the enemy. Why did that give him some hope?

"WHAT WAS THAT?" Maisy asked as soon as they were in her minivan.

"That was breakfast. Did you not like your pancakes?" Holly figured playing dumb was her best defense.

Maisy shook her head. "Don't even try to deny there is something going on between you and Jonah Drake. What was that I just watched happen between you two?"

"I don't know what you're talking about. That was us saying hello to someone we know. What do you think it was?"

"Why are you and Jonah joining Randall and Clarissa at the rodeo tomorrow?"

"I'm going with Randall and Old Red. Clarissa and Jonah just happen to be going as well."

"Okay, since when do you go to the Reindeer Rodeo with Randall and Old Red?"

"Since right now. Why do you care how I spend my time?"

"You haven't been to the rodeo since Randall retired. Not to mention it's hard to believe that Dad is letting you miss a shift at the Roadrunner to spend all day with Randall."

She was too smart for her own good. They had not told Maisy about the plan to stop the wedding because she was acting like it wasn't the end of the world. She had been offering to help Randall since he proposed.

"Dad is fine with me taking the day off. I have his full blessing."

"Does Dad know that the Drakes are going?"

"Dad could know a lot of things. He could also know nothing. I don't know what Dad knows." Holly clicked her seat belt into place and pulled down the visor, sliding the little cover to reveal the mirror. She checked to make sure her cheeks weren't red. She had felt them heat up when they were talking to Jonah.

Maisy finally turned the key in the ignition. "There is one of two things going on here. Either you and Dad are in cahoots with each other and are following Randall around in hopes that you can convince him not to get married, or you are secretly crushing on Jonah."

Holly flipped the visor up with some extra zip. "I am not crushing on Jonah. The only thing I feel for anyone with the last name Drake is resentment. Had Jonah's great-grandfather not reneged on his promise to compensate our great-grandfather with the piece of land they were selling, we could be living completely different lives right now."

"I don't think our lives are so bad. What do you wish was different? Now that you've spent a morning at the Coyote Social Club, you wish you had been a member all this time?"

"No," Holly said with a huff. "I would still be me just without having to worry every month if I'm going to be able to pay my bills."

Maisy checked her mirrors and turned her head to make sure it was safe to pull out into the road. "I think we all could benefit from a little reminder that we are extremely fortunate. We have roofs over our heads, food in our refrigerators and an amazing family that loves one another. Maybe if we focused on all we have instead of what we don't have, we could put the Hayward-Drake feud to bed once and for all. The people you have issues with aren't even the people who caused the rift in the first place. What bad things has Jonah ever done to you?"

This was exactly why they were not including Maisy in the plans. She did not get it. She forgot how the Drakes always looked down on them. Even Jonah. He could claim he didn't talk in a certain way to make her feel less, but that was exactly how she had felt.

"Whatever you say, Maisy. Let's all be one big, happy family. You should definitely do a toast at the wedding."

"I love you, Holly, but sometimes you are the queen of getting in your own way. Happiness is waiting for you if you'd let yourself experience it."

"Why are you so worried that I'm not happy? I am perfectly happy. I can be happy and not want Randall to marry into that family. I don't think the two things can't exist at the same time."

"You don't sound happy, Auntie Holly," Gia said from her booster seat in the back.

"You mad, Auntie," Patrick added.

Maisy smiled smugly from the driver's seat. "From the mouths of babes."

Holly was done trying to make her case. Partly because it was a little weak. If she was being honest, Jonah had some redeeming qualities. He had a way of making Holly drop her guard like he did on Saturday. It had rattled her when she had realized she was having so much fun with him that they were both becoming too comfortable around one another. That was why she had needed to get out of there as soon as possible.

She wouldn't admit it to Maisy, but Holly was fighting some real feelings and they were in direct conflict with how she thought she should feel, the way she had been proclaiming to the world that she felt. Moving forward, she needed to be more careful about her interactions with Jonah. They did not need to muddy the waters any more than they had already done.

"Can you drop me off at Mom and Dad's?" Holly asked as they turned off Main Street. Her dad would help set her straight. No one was more passionate about stopping this wedding than he was.

Holly's parents were both in the family room stretching out on yoga mats. This was her mom's new thing. Holly wasn't aware that she had convinced her dad to do it, too.

"Now breathe in slowly through your nose and then out through your mouth. Find your center," her mom instructed.

Will did as his wife said with his palms pressed together in front of his chest like he was praying. Her parents were complete opposites. Her dad was tall and bulky while her mom was small and wispy. She could fold herself into a tiny ball, and no one had ever used the word *tiny* to refer to anything related to her dad.

"You guys are so zen," Holly said, startling them.

"Hi, sweetie. To what do we owe the pleasure?" her mom asked, popping to her feet and giving Holly a hug.

Her dad was a bit less graceful and way less zen. "What's the matter? Is something wrong?"

"This is why you need to do yoga with me more often, Will. You're always so quick to stress out. I'm sure our daughter is here because she loves us and wanted to see us."

"I was going to see her in a few hours. Why are you here now? Please don't tell me

Randall ran off and eloped because there is not enough yoga in the world that will help me de-stress after that."

"I am unaware of any plans to elope. I was just coming back from breakfast with Maisy and the kids and thought I would stop by and talk to Dad about a couple things."

Her mom shook her head. "You two worry about work too much. When you are not at the bar, you need to enjoy being free."

"I'll stop worrying when we're retired and staring at the ocean every morning," he said as she started for the kitchen.

"If the worry doesn't get you first, dear! I'm going to make us some smoothies. Holly, you want anything, sweetheart?"

"I'm good, Mom."

"What are you really doing here?" her dad asked. "It isn't to talk about work, is it?"

"I just wanted to make sure that you were okay with me going to the rodeo with Randall tomorrow. I was thinking maybe this would be a good opportunity for you to help out with this plan of ours."

"I can't. I have to be here for some deliveries tomorrow, and I don't think I can be as good as you are at pretending that seeing the two of them together doesn't boil my blood."

"Maisy thinks we should be more accepting and stop living in the past. She thinks we'd be a lot happier if we accepted that not all Drakes are bad people."

Will dropped into his recliner. "Your sister takes after your mother. Thank goodness you are one hundred percent Hayward."

Holly was proud of being a Hayward, but she couldn't help feeling a little guilty about everything after seeing Randall and Clarissa together. When she added in Maisy's acceptance of this wedding, Holly was beginning to doubt herself. Now, it seemed her mother felt the same as Maisy. "So I'm guessing Mom thinks this is all a bad idea?"

"I have not exactly told your mother what we're doing. She knows I'm not happy about this wedding and she knows that I plan to protest."

"And…"

"And she thinks I'm being an obstinate fool and that I should support Randall in whatever decision he makes."

Holly stepped around the coffee table that had been moved for their yoga session. She began to roll up the yoga mats. She had to do the same with these doubts, roll them up and put them away. She tried justifying their plan. "That's why the plan is to see to it that Randall makes the right decisions all on his own."

The sound of the blender coming from the kitchen meant that her mom would not hear what they were talking about. Will stroked his beard. "I'm starting to get worried that there's not enough time to make that happen. They've been engaged for almost an entire week and he's still as happy about all this as he can be. We might need to think about other ways to disrupt this timeline."

"What did you have in mind?"

"You need to find out what the plans are. Where are they planning to get married? How are they inviting people to come to the wedding? Once we know these things, we can make it harder for them to happen."

"What do you want me to do? Check all the mailboxes in town and pull out the invites before they see them?"

"Not a terrible idea."

"Dad! That's literally a federal crime. I am not stealing mail from mailboxes." She set the rolled mats aside and pushed the coffee table back in place. "There's got to be something else we can do."

"What if you didn't steal them from mailboxes? What if you got them before they were mailed? No guests, no wedding. Maybe that would make them rethink things."

"Let me see what Jonah thinks."

Will blinked his eyes and tipped his head to the side. "And why would we need to run things past a Drake?"

It had been an automatic response. She was somehow living in a world where she wondered what Jonah thought before she wanted to act. She put the back of her hand on her forehead. Maybe she was sick. There was clearly something wrong with her.

"He's kind of like our inside man on the other side. Maybe he knows if they plan to send out invites. Clarissa is probably doing the wedding planning. Randall wouldn't know how to do any of that. He's just going to sign the checks."

"That's true. I'm sure she'll be asking him to sign lots and lots of checks. The Drakes love to take, take, take. Did I tell you about how Oliver and his buddies used to steal this one kid's lunch and it wasn't until me and my friends stood up to them that they stopped?"

She nodded. He had told her. They had been in elementary school. Kids do a lot of dumb things in elementary school. Holly had done some dumb things in elementary school. But her dad was sure that meant it was proof that Oliver had always been a bad seed.

It made her think about what Maisy said in the van earlier. What bad things had Jonah done to her? He had used fancy words to make her look stupid in front of other people when they were in high school. Of course, he used fancy words all the time. It wasn't like he only used them when she was around. The more Holly thought about the reasons she didn't like Jonah, the more she realized they had more to do with her insecurities than they did with him.

"Randall cannot marry into that family. We have to do what we can to stop it in the next two and a half weeks. I don't think I could be a part of his life anymore if he marries her. My dad, my grandpa—they would stop this."

Her mom came out of the kitchen holding two green smoothies. "Who would stop what?"

"I need to stop eating so unhealthy and listen to my beautiful wife more often."

Bonnie Hayward was no fool. She gave Holly a look that said he was full of it, but played along anyway. "I keep telling him that he will not starve to death if he has a salad for lunch every now and then."

Holly didn't want to let her dad down. She'd continue to try to set Randall up in situations that would expose relationship deal breakers. If this wedding wasn't meant to be, it would all work out like they hoped. If they couldn't convince him, then maybe Maisy and her mom were right. Only time would tell.

CHAPTER SEVEN

THURSDAY WAS OPENING day at the Reindeer Rodeo at the Delany Arena in the nearby rural town of Ranger. The three-day event was something Randall used to participate in and now attended as a spectator. Besides watching the rodeo events, visitors could shop vendors and snack on concessions, and, of course, there was a visit from Santa on the final day.

Holly hadn't been to the rodeo in several years, mainly because she was usually working. She had forgotten how much excitement they generated.

"Randall Hayward!" Not surprisingly there were lots of people who knew Randall. Buddy Dallas was one of the local circuit's popular bull riders.

The two of them spent a minute catching up before Randall introduced him to everyone else, including Clarissa, whom he referred to as his future wife.

As soon as they finished with Buddy there were five more people waiting to say hello to Randall. It was going to be hard to get to their seats if this kept up.

Jonah nudged Holly. "Do you want to…" He nodded his head toward the vendor selling cowboy hats.

Holly tapped Old Red's shoulder. "Jonah and I are going to go walk around. We'll meet you guys in the stands."

Old Red gave her a wink and a nod. Holly followed Jonah over to the hats. He picked up a black one and tried it on. "What do you think?"

She thought he looked kind of hot. There was no way she was telling him that. "Eh," she said, making a face.

He set it back on the table. "Never wear a hat. Got it."

"I wouldn't say *never* wear a hat." She picked up a brown leather hat and set it on his head. That one looked even better. "You could wear that one."

"This one?" He checked himself in the mirror. "Not bad."

Holly rolled her eyes. He had to know he was good-looking. "Maybe we should get your grandma a hat to go along with the Western outfit she's wearing today."

Holly had to give Clarissa a little credit. She had come dressed to impress. She had on blue jeans with a pink, white and gray flannel button-down underneath her winter jacket. The gray cowboy boots were the cherry on top. She definitely wanted to look like she'd been to the rodeo before.

"Be nice," Jonah warned.

"I think it's adorable actually. If she's trying to look the part of a rodeo wife, she's doing a great job." A great job of making it impossible for Holly to feel completely comfortable with her plan.

"We don't want her to be anyone's wife, remember?" He took off the hat and set it back down. He was right. They both wanted the same thing, so it couldn't be wrong.

"Let's hope she has a terrible time, then. Because this is Randall's world. He loves this life. All of his people are rodeo guys, as you can see."

Randall, Old Red and Clarissa were still

surrounded by people excited to see her great-uncle. Jonah seemed torn.

"She was nervous about coming. In fact, she woke up this morning wanting to cancel. She was going to tell him that she needed to do wedding planning and he should go without her."

"Good thing we had you there to push her to show up."

"Honestly, I almost let her back out."

"What? Why?"

Jonah's nose scrunched up. "I hate that she has to feel uncomfortable. She's my grandmother and she's the most gentle soul I know. She would never intentionally cause someone else discomfort."

It was sweet that he felt protective of her. "It's for a good cause, right? If we get them to back out now, we'll save them worse heartache later. We'll keep them from straining relationships with their families."

"That's what I keep telling myself. Otherwise, I'm a terrible grandson."

"You're thinking about the bigger picture, how this marriage impacts everyone in our families." She was justifying her own actions even more than his. Holly felt as guilty as Jonah. She had never seen Randall so happy. In the last week, he had put himself in two situations that were out of his comfort zone and made the best of them. At times, he looked like he was having fun.

Holly hadn't expected him to fit into those parts of Clarissa's world. If Randall was going to adapt so easily, she needed Clarissa to not fit into his. It might mean that Holly would lose the bet that Randall would back out before Clarissa, but so be it.

"Gran made an appointment at the Devonshire to reserve the space for the wedding and reception. I offered to go with her tomorrow, basically to make sure that they can't get married there. I'm hoping the more hassles she has trying to get everything done in the short time she's given herself, the more likely she'll be to at least postpone."

"Good idea. If they do find somewhere to have this thing, I was going to offer to mail the invitations and then not mail them, claiming they got lost in the mail."

"Also a good idea." Jonah's expression was still solemn. He glanced back at Randall and Clarissa. "Did you notice how he looks at her when he introduces her to someone? It's like he's presenting them to the Queen."

Holly had noticed. Randall had never looked at anyone the way he looked at Clarissa. As much as he had liked some women over the years, he never fell head over heels. This was different, and it only added to Holly's uncertainty.

Changing the subject was the best way to get her mind off these feelings. "It's almost the same way Janet Williams was looking at you at the gingerbread competition."

Jonah started to walk away. "You are ridiculous."

It put a smile on Holly's face to successfully make him uncomfortable. He made it too easy sometimes. "Oh, come on. The world needs to know why Dr. Jonah Drake is still single after all these years when there are so many ladies in Coyote swooning over him left and right."

"I'm going to find us some seats." He kept walking into the main arena.

"I know you think I'm teasing, but I'm serious about Janet telling me that she was hoping to hook up with you at the contest," she said, following him up the bleacher steps.

"No one goes to a gingerbread house contest trying to find a date."

"She didn't go to the contest to talk to you. She saw an opportunity when she realized you were there. She's not some kind of stalker. Janet was a pretty nice person from what I can remember."

"So the criteria for who I should date should be based on who you think might be nice?" He started down one of the aisles and sat down when he got in far enough so everyone else in their group would fit.

"Okay, what's your criteria? Maybe I know someone who will win the heart of Coyote's most eligible bachelor. Those were Janet's words, not mine," she clarified.

He turned to her with a skeptical look in his eyes. "Why are you suddenly so interested in my love life?"

"I'm not."

"Great, then let's talk about something else. How come you aren't married yet?" he asked, turning the tables.

"Nope."

"Oh, it's okay for you to ask about my dating life, but I can't ask about yours."

She decided not to shy away from the question like he did. She had nothing to hide and no reason to be embarrassed about choosing to be single at the moment. "Fine. I'm not married because I haven't met anyone I want to marry yet. It's pretty simple."

"What are you looking for that's so hard to find?"

He was really going to keep this up. Holly pushed her hair over her shoulder and put her feet up on the bleacher seat in front of her. "I don't have a set criteria. I mean, I would like him to have a job and not be a murderer."

"Wow," he replied with his eyebrows lifted. "Has it really been that difficult to meet people who fit those stringent guidelines?"

She rested her elbows on her knees. "You'd be surprised."

He chuckled and they sat in silence for a minute. The arena was buzzing with people taking their seats. Holiday music played over the loudspeakers. The contestants for the first event of the evening were gathered by the chute.

"I think I don't date a lot because work keeps me so busy and when I'm not working, I'm helping out around the ranch or taking care of something for my gran or my mom. I'm not good at making time for myself or a partner."

Holly was taken aback by his honesty. His self-evaluation resonated with her. They were very similar. "I can relate to that. When I'm not at the bar, I'm thinking about what I need to do at the bar to help my dad out. When I have time, I tend to spend it with my sister and her family because it's just easier. I don't have to do anything to get them to love me, you know what I mean?"

"I do. It's not always about finding someone who meets your criteria as much as it is about finding someone who thinks you meet their criteria."

Those were the cold, hard facts. "My sister married so young while I can't even keep a serious boyfriend. I started to think that maybe I should be like Randall and stay single my whole life, but now he's trying to mess me up by falling in love and getting married in his golden years."

"Doesn't that give you hope that you might not be as over the hill as you think?"

"Man, am I really going to have to wait until I'm in my eighties?"

Jonah put his hand on her back and it sent a shiver down her spine. He leaned in close, causing a heat to creep up her neck. "I'm confident that the employed nonmurderer who will fall for you is out there somewhere and you'll find him before you're eighty."

She turned her head ever so slightly and he was right there with that little grin on his lips. He had nice lips.

"You picked some good seats. We should have a good view from here," Randall said, coming up the aisle with drinks in his hands.

Jonah pulled away and Holly put her feet down, sitting upright. She took a shaky breath and tried to get her wits about her. Since when was it harder to not like a Drake than to like him?

JONAH WAS FAIRLY certain that Holly almost kissed him. Or maybe he almost kissed her. He wasn't sure what had just happened, but it was probably a good thing that his gran and Randall and his friend showed up.

All this talk about relationships and being loved was messing with his head. It had been a long time since he had spoken so openly about his feelings with someone. For some reason, Holly made it easy to be honest about things. She had this way of dropping her sarcasm shield and luring him in with this vulnerability that was wildly attractive.

"We got you guys a drink," his gran said, taking a seat next to Holly and passing her a cup. "Randall knows everyone here. They gave us all this for free."

"It's good we're here as Randall's guests," Jonah said as Holly passed the cup to him.

"Randall loves the rodeo," Holly said to Gran. "He goes whenever there's one in town. You'll be a rodeo queen once you two get married. Everyone will know you soon enough."

"That's going to take some getting used to. I'm not accustomed to being the center of attention." There was that discomfort that Jonah had been dreading.

Holly kept laying it on thick. "Well, you're going to have to get used to it. Randall doesn't know how to be anything but the center of attention. Always has been. And now that he's won the lottery, he always will be."

"That was a hot topic. No one can believe he won."

"Winning the lottery was nothing compared to winning your heart," Randall said, putting his arm around her. "You're what makes me the luckiest guy in the world."

Gran patted him on the knee and snuggled into him. He was good at making her feel special. That was going to be tough to discount.

"Do you enjoy coming to the rodeo?" Gran asked Holly.

"I like a good rodeo. Haven't been to one in a while, though."

"My grandniece works too much," Randall said. "I tell her dad all the time that he needs to make sure he doesn't work the poor girl to death."

"Sounds like my grandson. He'll work a full day, come home and work around the ranch for a couple hours, and then get called out on an emergency and be gone all night long helping someone's pregnant cow. I don't know when he sleeps or eats."

"No wonder you two have been getting

along so well these past couple days. You're cut from the same overworked cloth."

Jonah was surprised to hear that Randall thought they were getting along. Not that he could disagree. Jonah had been having more fun with Holly than anyone he'd spent time with in years.

"Yeah, I'm sure Jonah appreciates his work being compared to the work of a bartender."

"I wasn't comparing the work you do to the work he does," Randall explained. "I was talking about your work ethic. You don't have to be a doctor to be someone who works hard."

"I don't mind being compared to you, either," Jonah added. She didn't say anything but acknowledged him with a nod.

Until she had mentioned how she had felt back in high school, he never imagined that Holly ever felt inferior to anyone. She'd had this confidence about her that had been extremely intimidating when they were growing up. He would have described her as fearless.

"You want to know who works hard?"

Old Red said, chiming in. "The barrel racers coming up later tonight. My money is on Tanya Davis. I saw her last summer. She was incredible."

Randall disagreed and the two old men started arguing. Gran sat with her hands in her lap and the uncomfortable look was back on her face.

Holly leaned closer. "Are you very familiar with the different events?"

Gran shook her head. "I know there's some bucking broncos and bull riding."

Holly laughed lightly. "We don't call the event bucking broncos but yes, there is one for saddle bronc riding as well as bareback. Those and bull riding are part of the rough stock events. There are also timed events like the barrel racing, steer wrestling and roping. Now that these two guys aren't in the rodeo, Randall and Old Red like to bet on who is going to have the fastest times."

"What did you do when you worked for the rodeo?" she asked Randall.

"In my much younger days, I did some team roping events with this guy." He thumbed over his shoulder at Old Red. "I also did some bronc riding. I wasn't good enough to ride the bulls, but I did become a bullfighter for some other guys."

"A bullfighter? Like with the red cape?"

Old Red cackled so hard he almost fell out of his seat. Gran turned three shades of red.

"No, sweetheart. A bullfighter in the rodeo is part of the crew that protects the bull rider when he falls off the bull. Sometimes they call us rodeo clowns. We provide a little comic relief, but our main job is to keep that two-thousand-pound animal from trampling the fallen rider."

"That sounds horribly dangerous."

Randall held her hand. "Not when you know what you're doing."

"It's still dangerous," Holly contradicted him. "Randall loves a little danger."

"I have lived a long and happy life on my own terms. A little danger has been good for my soul."

"But you wouldn't be reckless. Not at your age, right?" Gran asked.

Randall did his best to assuage her fears. "You don't have to worry about me. I'm the guy with nine lives."

"Who's on his ninth," Old Red pointed out.

The announcer came over the speaker to welcome everyone and present the contestants for the first event. Five children stepped into the arena and waved.

Gran's worry only grew. "They're not going to let those small children ride in the rodeo, are they?"

"The first event tonight is Mutton Bustin'," Holly explained. Jonah remembered the first time he came to the rodeo with his dad and grandpa, Mutton Bustin' had been his favorite. He begged his dad to get him a spot in one but he had already been too big to compete.

"The kids ride a sheep sort of like the cowboys ride the bulls. They wear helmets and vests, Gran. Don't worry."

"This is the only event I have ever competed in," Holly said. "It's super safe and completely hilarious to watch. Wait for it."

"You got to be in a Mutton Bustin' event?"

"My great-uncle was a rodeo clown. Of course I got to be in the event. I was pretty good, too."

"I wanted to do that so badly. It looked so fun."

"It was. When you're five years old and

weigh forty pounds, riding that sheep feels like you're riding a bull. It's a thrill and a half."

"My money is on the girl in the pink hat," Old Red declared.

"I have five that says the boy in the chaps is definitely staying on all six seconds. He looks like he's been here before," Holly said.

"You're both wrong," Randall said. "It's clearly going to be the boy in the red shirt. He's got those long skinny legs. That'll help him hold on real tight."

"I think you're all wrong," Jonah said. "It is definitely going to be the girl who looks exactly the way I picture Holly looked when she was that age. The one with the shirt that says, 'Dear Santa, Define good.' That is so Holly."

"Maisy actually bought me a shirt that says that a couple years ago," she replied with a giggle.

"I knew it."

Randall continued to argue why his pick was going to win. Old Red gave all his reasons why that young man didn't have a chance. Randall tried to increase the bet to five hundred dollars, which Holly very quickly shot down. Jonah had to agree with her that not all of them could afford that bet.

"Well, then I guess I have to bet on the little guy in the Santa hat," Gran said unexpectedly.

Jonah and Holly exchanged surprised looks. Not only had she picked the smallest, youngest kid out there, it was so unlike her to get involved in betting.

"That's a terrible bet, Clarissa," Old Red warned. "That kid won't last a second if he even gets on the sheep at all when his turn comes up."

Jonah was sure that would discourage her from trying to participate in this friendly bet. He felt bad, but it was exactly what he and Holly needed her to do. Today was about getting her to see that she didn't fit in Randall's world.

"Well, I like to root for the underdog. Five and only five dollars on the boy in the Santa hat," she said, leaving Jonah even more stunned. She opened her purse and pulled out a five-dollar bill from her wallet.

"That's my girl," Randall said, looking more enamored than ever.

Holly's shoulders drooped. Every time

they took one step forward in this plan, Gran or Randall would do something that sent them two steps back. It was like they were some kind of match made in heaven.

The announcer thanked some sponsors and called everyone's attention to Chute Four. Some upbeat Christmas carol was playing in the background. "All right, first up, we've got Fancy Nancy coming your way riding Flash Gordon."

Randall pointed out that the men in the arena were there like bullfighters, to keep the kids safe when they fell off. Fancy Nancy was Old Red's pick for staying on longest. She had traded her pink hat in for a pink helmet. They got her on the sheep and the gate was opened.

Fancy Nancy was sitting straight up on that sheep and as soon as that animal realized it had someone on its back, it kicked its back legs up and Fancy Nancy fell right off.

Old Red threw his rodeo program down in disgust. "Oh man. Come on, Fancy Nancy! The first rule of Mutton Bustin' is lay down. Lay down and hold on for dear life."

She was awarded eighty points since she had a bucker. Next up was Jonah's choice.

Her name was Ella and she was riding Sheepbob Squarepants. The gate opened and Ella had perfect form. Her legs were wrapped tightly around the sheep and she was gripping that wool for dear life.

"Whoa, man. Ella is hanging on!" the announcer shouted and Ella and her sheep took off across the arena. She showed no signs of flopping. In fact, she was clearly going to make it all the way across. "She's headed for the concession stand!" The announcer's joke made the crowd laugh.

Ella held on until the sheep turned around and started to zigzag on its way back from where it came from. She fell but received a roaring cheer. She ended up with a score of ninety-five.

Jonah felt justified in gloating. "I knew my Holly look-alike would pay up."

"Hang on there, Mr. Big Shot. We still have a few more contestants to go," Holly reminded him.

"Next up, we have Bo. Big Bo is going to be riding Dasher. Let's hear it for Big Bo!"

Bo was Gran's choice, and as soon as that gate opened, it was obvious that Bo had no intention of hanging on to his sheep. The bullfighter snatched him right off the sheep's back before he could fall and get hurt.

"Hey, they didn't let him ride," Gran complained.

"They were doing their job, sweetheart," Randall explained. "Had they let him go much further, he would have been thrown off the back and might have landed on his head."

"Told ya. That was a terrible bet," Old Red said just as they were reading off the score. Somehow, Bo received the same score as Miss Fancy Nancy. "What? How can someone who didn't even ride the sheep out of the chute get the same score as my kid who got bucked off?"

"Guess you both are terrible betters. I think you owe my fiancée an apology," Randall said, giving his friend an elbow to the gut.

Old Red hung his head. "Sorry, Clarissa."

"Hopefully, we'll both have better luck next time," she said gracefully. Jonah couldn't help but feel proud of her for holding her own with that old coot.

"Next, we welcome Grady riding Dasher's

sister Prancer. Let's see how that goes," the announcer said.

Randall's rider was well prepared. Grady did wrap his long legs around the sheep, but Prancer was quick and liked to move from side to side instead of running in a straight line. First, Grady slid over to the right and was hanging off the side. Prancer gave him one more jiggle and the boy landed on the dirt.

Gran and Randall had been cheering so loudly. She was quick to comfort him when Grady's score came back a ninety. Close, but not enough to beat Jonah.

"I guess you're the last woman standing," Jonah said to Holly.

"You're going down, Dr. Drake. You and Ella and Sheepbob are going down."

"Next up, we have Jonah riding Sheepa Claus."

Gran loved it. "Can you believe that you picked someone named Jonah and he picked the little girl who reminded him of you? That's so funny! Now I don't know who to root for."

Holly didn't have time to say anything before little Jonah in his leather chaps took off on Sheepa Claus. The kid was a total pro. Holly had read him perfectly. He had the positioning down and his sheep ran in a perfect line across the arena. The sheep turned around when it got close to the group of sheep that were still out there from the previous rounds. Little Jonah still hung on. When he went racing by, one of the bull-fighters snatched him off.

"Way to go, Jonah! What a ride by that little fellow," the announcer cheered him on. "The judges give Jonah a ninety-four. That's a ninety-four."

Holly went from ready to celebrate her win to shocked into silence.

"What?" Randall exclaimed.

"Well, that's not right. He didn't fall off. They took him off," Gran noted.

"These judges are just throwing numbers out there. I don't even think they remember what they gave the kid before," Old Red complained.

Holly finally spoke. "Maybe they gave some extra points for difficulty. Ella had to hold on to a much wilder sheep than Little Jonah. Our Jonah wins fair and square. Everyone pay up."

Jonah collected his twenty dollars, but his real win was getting called "our Jonah" by Holly. It might not have meant anything to her, but it made him feel like she was beginning to welcome him into her very tight circle, and that was something.

CHAPTER EIGHT

RANDALL AND CLARISSA were never going to break up before the wedding. As much as Holly believed that their differences would win out in the end, that was just not reality. In fact, the more time they spent together, the more in love with each other they got. Even worse, Holly was more confused than ever about her feelings for Jonah. She found herself looking forward to the next time they'd see each other and missed him when they were apart. That was how bad things had gotten.

Today, Holly was standing on Clarissa's front porch with her mom, her aunt Yvonne and her sister. In her arms, she held the bowl of cut-up fruit that her mother had insisted they bring to this little lunch at the Drakes' ranch.

Clarissa answered the door with such genuine gratitude in her voice. "Thank you all for coming, I really appreciate it."

"Thank you for inviting us. We're happy to be here," Holly's mom said. "We brought some fruit salad." She gave Holly a push forward.

Holly held out the bowl and Clarissa took it. "Thank you. You didn't have to bring anything, but this looks delicious." She stepped back and welcomed them inside.

Clarissa had arranged this luncheon to include the women from her family and the women from Randall's family. Waiting inside the house in the sitting room were Jonah's mother, his cousin and his aunt. Nancy, Jonah's mom, took their coats.

"Bonnie, let me introduce you," Clarissa said. "You know my daughter-in-law Nancy. This is my other daughter-in-law, Stacy. And this lovely lady is my granddaughter Julia."

"Hi, everyone. These are my daughters, Maisy and Holly. And this is Yvonne. She's married to Randall's sister's son, Frank."

Holly knew Julia Drake. She was a few years older than her and Jonah. She had two brothers who both moved out of state after they graduated. She had been at the tree-lighting ceremony and was congenial. Clarissa's decision to get the women together had to be due to the fact that they were much more open to the idea of the two families coming together than the men were. Or, like in Holly's case, they were better at hiding how they really felt.

"Can we get you something to drink? We have lemonade and iced tea," Nancy offered.

"Or if you need something to take the edge off, we do have some sangria," Julia said, holding up her cup.

Holly would have loved to take the edge off, but opted for the lemonade. Being around Jonah's family without Jonah was more stressful than she had expected. She didn't realize how much having him around put her at ease. They all took a seat on the couches and chairs, sipping their lemonades and iced teas.

"I thought it would be nice to get us all together so you all heard about the wedding plans at the same time." Clarissa pulled out a notebook and put her reading glasses on. "Jonah and I have a meeting tomorrow at the Devonshire. We're hoping we can do the ceremony and reception there. It's already decorated for the holidays, so we wouldn't have to buy any flowers except my bouquet and his boutonniere."

"I can talk to Sylvie at the flower shop downtown about putting those together," Nancy offered.

"Perfect. Thank you, dear. Once I know for sure the Devonshire can accommodate us on Christmas, I have the invitations ready to print. I wanted to keep things small, but Randall has a lot of friends, so it might be a little bigger than I expected."

Holly would have to talk to Jonah about how to use their differing idea of how many people should be invited to their advantage.

"Is there anything we can do to help?" Mom asked.

"I could mail out the invites for you," Holly jumped in. She needed to hijack the invitations per the plan.

"I appreciate that. I know all of this is happening very quickly, so we want to keep things as simple as possible. I don't want to make too much work for anyone. We just want our families to have a fun night and to simply get along."

That was all, huh?

"We love Randall and I am sure your family feels the same about you," Maisy said. "We will do what we have to do to make your day special."

"So we're all going to pretend like the men in this family aren't planning to protest?" Julia asked, dropping all the pretenses that everyone was ready to join hands and sing "Kumbaya."

"No one in our family is planning to protest," Mom said, painfully unaware of the fact that Holly's dad for sure planned to protest if this wedding wasn't stopped.

"My husband, Frank, and his dad love Randall. They just want him to be happy," Yvonne replied either unaware of how Frank actually felt or completely lying.

"That's what we all want. Right, girls?" her mom asked.

Holly's shoulders stiffened. She didn't want to straight-up lie to everyone here, but she also couldn't give away their true feelings if she wanted to stop this wedding from happening. It was probably better to say nothing at all. She glanced at her sister.

Maisy uncrossed and recrossed her legs. She hated lying. "Honestly, our dad still has some feelings to resolve about the matter, but I think we can get him to be accepting by Christmas," she said, giving Clarissa some majorly false hope. Holly knew that her sister absolutely believed what she said, but Holly also knew that was not happening. Their dad would not be accepting of this union by Christmas this year or ten years from now.

Julia was much more realistic. "Gran, I wish I could say that my dad is going to come around, but I don't know if we can get him to come around by Christmas."

Clarissa's face fell. "Well, I might need to have a heart-to-heart with Oliver. He is entitled to his feelings, but I need him to respect mine as well."

"What about Jonah? Jonah is fine with everything?" his aunt Stacy asked.

Holly knew his mom was well aware of how he truly felt. She watched her to see what she would say. Clarissa spoke up first.

"He's been very supportive. He's been helping me with what I need to do to prepare. He's been open to getting to know Randall. He wishes we weren't trying to get all this done by Christmas, but he has been on my side. Hasn't he, Nancy?"

Holly's gaze shifted to Nancy, who was cool as a cucumber. "He has been very hands-on with everything."

It was a very neutral response that gave none of his feelings away. Holly could breathe easy.

"Then it sounds like Oliver is the only one who needs a major talking-to," Clarissa concluded. "Why don't we eat some lunch and get to know one another a little better."

Holly felt that familiar guilt. Clarissa was a nice person. As much as she wanted to not like her because of whom she had been married to, the woman made it hard to do so.

"I heard Gran had the time of her life at the rodeo on Friday," Julia said as they all took a seat around the dining room table.

She'd had much more fun than Jonah or Holly had expected. Just like Randall, she was open to these new experiences and found ways to make the best of a situation. It was making Holly and Jonah's job impossible.

"I think she enjoyed it in the end," Holly said. "She should never bet at a rodeo, though. Her lack of rodeo experience shines through in her bets."

"Gran was betting?" Julia's jaw dropped. "Gran, is Randall turning you into a gambler? Dad is not going to like that."

"I'll be sure to add that to our list of things to discuss," Clarissa replied.

"It wasn't serious betting," Holly clarified. "We each picked a kid to cheer for during the Mutton Bustin' event. It was very innocent."

"Randall is really into gambling, isn't he?" Stacy asked.

"He enjoys it," Maisy answered.

Holly felt defensive. Her hackles rose. "And because of it, he now has enough money to gamble as much as he'd like."

"Oh, I know. I just hope he doesn't gamble all his lottery winnings away," Stacy said. "I think that's my husband's biggest concern. The Haywards have a history of not..." She stopped and Holly could feel the tips of her ears burning.

"A history of not what? Not having money? Not being rich like you Drakes?"

"Holly," her mom said. Her eyes pleaded with her to stop.

"Well, that's true, isn't it? The Drakes have worked very hard for what they have and Oliver wants to make sure that what his dad and his brother worked for stays in the family."

"Mom." Julia sounded exasperated just like Holly's mom.

"No one from our family has any intention of touching any of your precious money," Holly snapped. "And by the way, we have also worked very hard for everything we have and I don't appreciate you insinuating that we have not."

"I just meant we didn't win our money in the lottery."

Holly's whole face was hot. Her fingernails dug into her palms as she squeezed them into tight fists. "Randall won some money, but we have supported ourselves in this town for generations without the help of family money being handed down to us like your husband."

"My husband works harder than anyone in this entire state. He has grown his empire separate from his family's ranch," Stacy said, getting to her feet.

"Okay, that's enough!" Clarissa stood up

as well. "We will not do this. There is no reason for it and I will not tolerate it."

The sound of the front door opening and closing caught Holly's attention and suddenly Jonah stood in the doorway of the dining room. "Well, good afternoon, ladies."

Holly couldn't sit there and pretend that she was fine with breaking bread with them. "Excuse me," she said as she exited the room.

MAISY GOT UP out of her seat, but Jonah stopped her. "Let me," he said.

Holly hadn't been honest with her sister about her feelings or her plans. She might not be able to completely open up to her, so Jonah followed Holly outside.

"What's the matter? What did I do?"

"It's not you. It's your aunt. That woman is the reason why I am desperate to get Randall out of this engagement."

He could only imagine what his aunt Stacy had said or done. She and Uncle Oliver were of the same mind. "What did she do?"

"Oh, your aunt and uncle are very afraid that Randall is going to gamble all his lottery winnings away and have to dig into your grandmother's pockets to pay off his future gambling debts." She was so hot with anger that she kept pacing in front of him with her hands balled into fists. "Not to mention that he might turn her into a gambler and she might gamble all your dad's and grandfather's hard-earned money away. I assume that's an issue because then Oliver won't get his full inheritance."

Something had told him to come home for his lunch break. It was a good thing he had because there was no telling what Holly would have done otherwise. "Oliver has his misconceptions. Just like you have yours. Remember you were the one who called me up saying you were not going to let my grandmother take your great-uncle's money the night they got engaged. Do you think that his money has anything to do with why my gran loves him?"

That got her to cool her jets. She stopped pacing and rubbed her hands together. "No, but in my defense, I was in shock that night. We had no idea that they had been secretly dating. She just showed up at the bar. None of it made sense. I reacted without thinking."

"I know."

"What your aunt was implying is what has been the crux of this feud from the beginning. They think they are better than us. That the Hayward family is a bunch of poor, lazy, gambling fools." The fire was back.

Her pride had been wounded and he knew that was her Achilles' heel. He took her by the hand. "You are not a fool. You are not lazy. You do like a good bet and I have no idea how rich or poor you are. But you are no different than us. My aunt and uncle might not see that yet, but they will."

She pulled her hand away. "I don't care what they think. I just want to stop this wedding. I will stop this wedding. No matter what it takes."

"We'll do our best, but no matter what, I want you to know that Oliver and Stacy don't speak for everyone with the last name Drake. Just remember that, okay?"

She nodded. She took a deep breath, tipping her face up to the sun and closing her eyes. He watched as she calmed herself down.

"I should go back in and finish lunch before my mother and sister die of embarrassment."

"You did the right thing by stepping away. Nothing good was going to come from you and my aunt Stacy continuing to go at it."

"Your grandmother was not happy with either of us. You walked in right after she shut the conversation down."

Jonah knew it must have taken a lot to get his gran angry enough to snap. Hopefully while he had been out here with Holly, she'd had some words with Stacy.

"I'm going to join this little luncheon. I know you don't need me to defend you, but I think that if Stacy tries to get into it with you again, it would be a good idea for you not to take the bait. I will shut her down, I promise."

"Fine," she said with a heavy sigh. "Why are you being so nice to me? Shouldn't you be taking their side?"

"Not if their side is wrong, and they are wrong about you not being good enough to associate with us. We all put our pants on one leg at a time."

Finally, Holly smiled. "You have always talked like an old man. Even when you were a kid."

The wind blew her hair around. He reached

up and brushed some strands out of her face. That familiar urge to pull her close and kiss her was back. This feeling had been keeping him up at night this week.

It was strange to feel so protective of her while knowing she was one woman who didn't need anyone to protect her. She was more than capable of taking care of herself, so instead, he wanted to be the one who was there to remind her of that whenever she doubted.

"You like the way I talk. Admit it."

Her eyes were locked on his. He wished he could read her mind. "I actually wished you were home when I first got here. I don't know how I feel about the fact that I like having you around. Let's not push me to admit I like the way you talk, too."

That little confession sent his heart into overdrive. Falling for Holly Hayward had to be the dumbest thing he could ever do. That probably wasn't going to stop him from doing it, though.

As soon as they opened the door to go back inside, his grandmother was there to check on them.

"I apologize for my daughter-in-law, Holly.

I need you both to know that Randall and I have already talked about our money. Neither one of us wants money to be what comes between the people we love. We have agreed that the smartest thing to do is to keep our finances separate. I'm sorry I didn't mention it right away. I feel like that clarification could have saved us from that unfortunate argument."

It would make Oliver happy to know that they had come to that conclusion. Jonah wished he could figure out how to use what just happened to get Gran to see that the best thing would be to keep these two families separate. He was beginning to feel like a giant hypocrite. How could he push his gran away from the man she loved because of his last name but be pining for someone with that same last name?

Things were getting really complicated.

Holly accepted Gran's apology and rejoined the lunch. The room was painfully quiet. Jonah sat across from Holly.

"What's on the menu?" he asked.

Julia lifted her glass. "I suggest you start with some sangria. The lemonade and tea only led to awkward conversations."

"We have a variety of salads and sandwiches. Please, everyone, eat," Gran said, taking her seat at the head of the table.

"Gran says you're going with her tomorrow to check out the wedding venue," Julia said once the food had been passed around.

"I am. You want to come with us?"

"I'm surprised Holly's not going with you. You two seem to be joining Gran and Randall for everything."

"You're the one who backed out of the gingerbread contest this year."

Julia smiled. She had to know by now that Jonah would not be baited so easily. "We had a travel basketball tournament. The kids were disappointed they weren't there."

"Maybe you can come to the Frontier Freeze this weekend. Randall runs in with his pals every year," Holly suggested.

"He does the Frontier Freeze at his age? That's wild. I don't think I could convince my husband to do that. Are you doing it or just going to watch Randall?"

"I'm watching," Jonah answered at the same time that Holly said, "I'm doing it."

"You're doing it?" Jonah thought they were just going for moral support.

"You're not? What's the point of going and just watching other people run in?"

"What are you young people talking about down there?" Gran asked.

"The Frontier Freeze. Jonah says he's too chicken to go in while Holly is literally cold-blooded and totally doing it," Julia replied.

"Jonah, if I'm going in, you have to go in with me," Gran said, much to everyone's surprise.

"Clarissa, you cannot do the Frontier Freeze. You'll…freeze," Nancy said.

"It's not that bad," Holly's mom said. "Will and I did it years ago. You run in and run out. You're only cold for a couple seconds."

"Mother, that is totally a lie. Holly and I did it when I turned sixteen," Maisy said. "I remember being very cold, and it's impossible to warm up fast after getting in water that cold. It took my body the entire day to get to normal."

Holly shook her head. "It was not that bad. You are such a drama queen."

"I am not! I probably was close to getting freezer burn."

Jonah didn't mean to laugh, but he couldn't

stop and neither could anyone else at the table. "I think you mean frostbite," he said, hoping she wouldn't be too embarrassed.

Maisy luckily had a wonderful sense of humor and was quick to laugh at herself as well. "Oh my gosh. Frostbite. That's what I almost had."

"I'm not worried about frostbite or freezer burn," Gran said, refilling her glass of lemonade. "Randall says it's fun."

"Randall also thinks getting in an arena with a bucking bull is fun. I don't know if he's the best judge of what's entertaining for everyone," Jonah reminded her.

"You really don't like being cold, huh?" Holly asked, cocking a brow.

"Who likes being cold? We are humans, not polar bears."

"That's an automatic forfeit and a win for me, then."

Julia interrupted, "A forfeit? What kind of game are you two playing?"

"Holly likes to win things. Everything we do becomes some kind of competition."

"My win at the Freeze means we're back to being tied—two to two."

"You beat Holly at two competitions?" Julia looked impressed.

"You lost two competitions to Jonah?" Maisy was clearly shocked.

"He can ice-skate better, I decorate gingerbread houses better, and he got lucky and chose the best sheep rider."

"Wow, you two are really having some fun together," Julia said before taking another drink. "You can't bail on the Freeze. If Gran is doing it, you have to do it."

"There is no shame in forfeiting," Maisy said, kindly giving him an out. "Trust me, my sister will stay in that river until she turns blue just to win."

That didn't surprise him to hear. "I think I'm better off being in charge of handing you guys warm towels when you get out."

"That's very sweet of you, honey," Gran said.

They finished eating, and Jonah helped his mom and aunt take dishes into the kitchen. He really needed to get back to work. The luncheon ended much better than it started.

His grandmother walked into the kitchen to grab the desserts she had made. "Are you ready for some dessert?"

"I've got to get back to work, Gran. Hopefully there will be some left when I get home tonight," he said.

"I'll make sure we save you some."

"Here, Clarissa. We can take this out for you." Jonah's mom and aunt helped with the dessert.

Gran hung back as the two ladies returned to the dining room. "I just wanted to thank you for showing up. Without you, I don't know that I could have saved this lunch."

"No problem, Gran. I didn't do much."

"Things are always more fun when you're around. You and Holly make me laugh every time. I really enjoy spending time with you two."

"Well, I enjoy spending time with you, Gran."

"I think Holly enjoys when you're around. She always has a smile on her face when you're near. I notice these things."

Jonah wasn't sure where she was going with this. "I have to get back to work, Gran. I'll see you later. Thank you for lunch."

"You know I'm right," she said as he backed away. "I love you."

Jonah walked through the dining room

and announced a general goodbye. Holly looked up from her dessert plate and gave him a little wave before rejoining the conversation between Maisy and Julia.

Would it be so bad if these two families spent time together? What if he could convince Oliver that things were going to be all right? Jonah sure wouldn't mind more time with Holly. He glanced over his shoulder as he walked out. He caught her watching him and his heart took off running for the second time today. Stupid heart.

CHAPTER NINE

THE DEVONSHIRE HOTEL was located in the historic section of downtown Coyote in between the library and the one and only bank in town. Boasting thirty-five rooms and the largest banquet hall in all of Coyote, it was a popular choice for people looking to throw a fancy soiree.

The burgundy entrance canopy was draped in lighted garland and two eight-foot toy soldiers stood guard on either side. Jonah held the door open for his grandmother and they entered the lobby. Gran was wowed by the massive Christmas tree in the middle of the room. It was covered top to bottom in red and gold.

"I haven't been here in so long, I forgot what an amazing job they do for the holidays," she said.

It was lovely, but Jonah's goal today was to make sure they did not book the Devonshire for the wedding and reception. They went to the counter and asked for Megan, the event manager. They had a three o'clock appointment.

Megan came out of the back office with literal bells on. She had jingle bell earrings that jangled with every step. "Welcome to the Devonshire. Why don't you come on back to my office and we can get an idea of what you're looking for."

She brought them back and offered them some water. Her office was decorated like they were inside Santa's workshop. There were wrapped presents stacked in every corner and a bookcase filled with traditional kids' toys. A mailbox with "Letter to Santa" written on the side stood beside her desk. Behind her was a sign that displayed the names of the good and bad boys and girls. Megan loved Christmas.

Megan sat down and folded her hands in front of her on the desk. "So, you're planning a Christmas wedding."

"We are, and we're hoping you can accommodate us," Gran said.

"And you are the groom?" Megan asked

Jonah, clearly misreading the situation completely.

"No, I am the grandson. My lovely grandmother here is the bride."

"Oh! Well, how exciting. I would love to show you the space we have and then we can talk about the different packages we have available. Now, because it is such short notice, some of the options are going to be limited. We also charge an extra fee for holidays."

"Money is no object," Gran replied. That was the first time Jonah had heard her speak like someone marrying a millionaire.

"Great, then let's go look at the room, shall we?" Jingle Megan led them to their famous banquet room.

The space was gorgeous. It had dramatic high ceilings, ornate pillars and gold-painted trim work, and it was also decorated with thousands of lights, garland and ornaments.

"We can seat up to a hundred people. You can choose if you want there to be a banquet-style table for the wedding party or all round tables depending on how small or large your wedding party is."

Gran was completely enamored. He could

see that she was already envisioning her wedding happening right here. Jonah had no idea how he was going to stop this from happening. He should have had Holly come with them. Maybe she could have come up with something. He texted her that there was no way Gran wasn't going to pick this place.

Megan went on to describe the different packages available on such short notice. Gran was ready to sign on the dotted line. Holly texted back that he needed to keep her from signing and find a way to get another appointment so she could meet with the event planner.

"Why don't we go back home and think about it, Gran? We can call Megan tomorrow and let her know what we've decided."

"I've decided, Jonah. This place is perfect."

"What about Randall? Don't you think that before we make any final decisions, we should ask him what he thinks?" he asked.

"He told me he was fine with whatever I want," Gran said. Jonah was sure she wasn't going to back down, but then she said, "But I think you're right. We should include him in the process. He's never had a wedding. I want to make sure this one is just how he imagined it."

On their way out, Megan went back to her office to grab some paperwork for them to review. Gran stopped to use the restroom. Megan came back and handed Jonah a folder. He took the opportunity to talk to Megan alone.

"Would it be okay if I brought someone else to see the room before we decide?"

"Of course. Do you have any idea when you might come back?"

Jonah texted Holly. She replied she could come back with him today if he wanted. "Later today?"

"That's perfect. I'm here until five. Just give me a call when you're on your way."

Gran returned and she thanked Megan for her help and let her know she'd get back to her as soon as possible. Jonah took her home and let her tell his mom all about it. She called Randall and asked him to come by the ranch to go over the different options with her. Thankfully, he was busy until later that evening.

Jonah texted Holly that he was coming to get her and made up an excuse to leave the house. He went straight to the Roadrunner to get his partner in crime.

HOLLY FINISHED PREPPING the garnishes and went back into the kitchen to tell her dad she was leaving for an hour to help Jonah.

Will wasn't happy that Jonah couldn't handle this one thing on his own, but if it meant they successfully stopped them from securing a wedding venue, then he was going to let her go.

"Do what you gotta do. We're running out of time. If all we can do now is make it more difficult for this wedding to happen, then that's what we have to do, Hol."

There were a lot of conflicting feelings battling it out inside her over this wedding. She knew for a fact that there were some Drakes who looked down on all the people in her family and that did not sit well with her. It was one of the reasons her dad was so against this engagement, too. She was also well aware that Clarissa was not like that. She was kind and she honestly cared about Randall. It also seemed as if Clarissa wanted nothing more than to be accepted by Randall's family and friends.

Things would have been so much easier if she was related to any other family in Coyote. Just like Jonah. Holly felt just as confused about him lately. He could be nice. He could be funny. He could be exactly what Holly was looking for in a guy. But he was a Drake. His uncle thought people like her were trash. That was going to be a problem.

Her phone pinged with a text. Jonah was outside waiting to take her to the Devonshire. She wasn't exactly sure her plan was going to work, but she felt like she needed to try.

"I completely failed in my mission to shut this down," Jonah said when she got in his truck. "She was in love with the place before we even went inside. She's been there before. She just needed to know what they could do on short notice."

"Well, let's make the Devonshire not love the idea of hosting a Drake/Hayward wedding."

"And how do you plan on doing that?"

"I'm going to be the kind of Hayward your uncle and aunt think I am."

The crease between Jonah's eyebrows told

her he had no idea what she meant. He was about to find out.

As soon as they walked inside the Devonshire, Holly knew why Clarissa wanted to get married there. It was classy like she was. It also did Christmas in a spectacular way.

Jonah went to the front desk to ask for someone named Megan. When Megan came out to greet them, Holly was mesmerized by the jingle bells hanging from her ears.

"Megan, this is Holly. She's from the groom's side of the family."

"Hi, Megs. We just have a few questions. Number one, can we bring a horse into the banquet hall?"

Megan's face completely blanched. "No, ma'am, you cannot bring a horse into the hotel." She looked at Jonah. "Is she kidding?"

Holly could tell that Jonah wasn't sure what the correct answer was to that question so she saved him.

"I do not kid when it comes to horses. My great-uncle worked the rodeo circuit for forty years. We are going to have a lot of rodeo friends at this wedding. It's sort of a tradition that when the groom has ties to the rodeo, he rides into the reception on a horse."

"For real?" Megan still didn't seem sure if she was joking or not.

There was no such tradition in the rodeo world, but clearly Megan did not associate with anyone who was from that world. "For real. Is this going to be a problem? It's not like the horse stays the whole time. He rides it in, it does a loop around the room, poses for a few pictures, and then it goes home. Can you accommodate that?"

Megan's mouth hung open in disbelief. "No, we cannot accommodate that. Animals are not allowed."

"I didn't see that in the contract," Jonah said, finally catching on to what Holly was doing. "Do you have it in writing that animals are not allowed?"

"Sir..." Megan seemed flustered. "I don't know if it's in the paperwork I gave you, but this hotel has a no-pet rule."

"But that's for guests staying at the hotel, right?" Holly asked. "We wouldn't be guests of the hotel. The horse doesn't need a room for the night or anything."

"We cannot let you bring a horse into any part of the hotel. I'm very sorry."

Holly pivoted. "What about a mechanical bull? If it's not alive, is it okay if we set up a mechanical bull on the dance floor?"

"A mechanical bull?"

"Are there outlets near the dance floor or do you have extension cords we could borrow or would we need to bring our own?" Jonah asked.

Megan shook her head back and forth, causing her earrings to ring nonstop. "I am not sure you can have a mechanical bull."

"Who do you need to clear that with and how long will it take you to get back to us about that because if we can't have a horse, we're going to want the bull for sure. It requires us to rent a very large truck, though, and I need to have enough time to make sure they can get it here."

"Would people be riding the bull?"

Holly let out an exaggerated laugh. "Meggy, what good is a mechanical bull if no one can ride it? For sure people are going to be riding it and I am going to make sure you fall off in like two seconds, Jonah."

"Oh, I can stay on for longer than two seconds."

"Yeah, right. I will bet you a hundred bucks that with me behind the controls, I will have you off that bull in one second or less."

Megan cleared her throat. "I feel like that would be a huge liability issue for the hotel. I don't think we can have people riding a mechanical bull on our property. If someone were to get hurt, we just couldn't have that."

"Well, hang on there. So you're telling me that I can't have a horse or a bull. Alive or not. What about BYOB? Are we allowed to bring our own booze?"

"I'm sorry." Megan looked like she was going to be sick. "I feel like there has been a major miscommunication. The room is for rent along with a dinner, music and bar package. There is no outside food or drinks allowed. There can be no animals. There can be no dangerous activities while you are on our premises."

Holly huffed and threw her hands up and let them slap loudly against her legs. "So we're going to have two hundred people come to this wedding and we can't have any of those things."

"Our room's capacity is only one hundred people."

"Yeah, but it's not like you're going to have bouncers at the door. If a couple extra people show up, you can't make them leave, right?"

Jonah did a good job maintaining a straight face. "If they have to kick people out, it's going to be the people from your side, not ours. My grandmother has a very specific list of people she wants at the wedding and we will not turn any of her friends away."

Holly raised her voice, getting the attention of some of the guests checking into the hotel. "Oh, but my great-uncle shouldn't be allowed to celebrate the biggest day of his life with his friends and family? All of them?"

"We both know that most of your uncle's friends are hooligans who are known for destroying places when they are all in a room together."

"It's called having fun! Maybe you should try it for once."

"Yeah, well, I prefer the kind of fun that doesn't get me arrested, but I'm pretty sure all the parties your family has thrown have ended with the police showing up for one reason or another."

"It's not a good party if it doesn't get shut down by the police!"

"Excuse me," Megan interrupted their fake fight. Her face was bright red and her jingle bell earrings were angrily ringing. "Please stop yelling at each other in our lobby. Please stop."

"Sorry. You have no idea what it's been like trying to plan this wedding with this woman and her family."

"I don't think we can help you. It sounds like you need a bigger space than we can provide and that there are several issues that make us the wrong choice for the kind of event that you want to have. I am sorry, but we cannot rent you the space. Please tell your grandmother that I am very sorry."

"You're refusing to sign a contract with us?"

"Based on the number of people you want at this wedding, we cannot accommodate you. So, yes, we are refusing to sign a contract with you."

Jonah apologized and thanked her for her time. Holly kept up the act and continued to shout at him for wasting *her* time by finding a place that once again didn't allow horses or have enough space for all of Randall's friends.

As soon as they got outside, Jonah turned around and picked Holly up off her feet. He spun her around. "You are so freaking amazing. I don't know how you came up with that, but that was the most brilliant thing I have ever seen in my entire life."

He set her down but didn't let her go. Holly felt dizzy, but she wasn't sure it was from being spun around.

"Your acting skills are pretty good, too. I was impressed that you caught on so quickly."

"We are a good team." Jonah reached up and gently cupped her cheek.

Holly felt like she couldn't breathe. The way he looked at her caused her whole body to freeze. He leaned in closer and she was incapable of backing away. Not that she wanted to back away. She wanted to be right there, in his arms for as long as he'd have her.

Slowly, he tipped her head up and bent his down until their lips connected. He kissed her as if he had been waiting to do that as long as she had. Holly found herself wrapping her arms around his neck and kissing him back.

When he stopped kissing her, reality set in. She kissed Jonah Drake. There was no way that could be a good idea. She unlinked her hands and took a step back, breaking his hold on her.

"I need to get back to the Roadrunner. My dad needs my help."

Jonah's expression went from pleased to concerned in a flash. "I didn't mean to—"

Holly cut him off. "It's really important that I get back. We've celebrated one win. There's still a lot to do to get this wedding called off."

He cleared his throat and shoved his hands in his jacket pockets. "Right. Let's get you back."

Holly followed him to the truck and tried to force herself to stop thinking about the way her lips still tingled from being caressed by his. Unfortunately, she'd be thinking about that kiss for the rest of her life.

CHAPTER TEN

"WHO'S READY TO get cold?" Maisy and the kids shouted out the minivan windows as Holly stepped outside. As was tradition, they were coming to watch Auntie Holly and Great-Uncle Randall go running in the icy river.

"Me!" Holly waved her hand in the air as she ran toward the vehicle. "Who's ready to cheer for Auntie Holly when she turns into an ice cube?"

"Me!" Gia and Patrick said in unison as Holly climbed in the back with them.

"Who thinks Mommy should jump in the river, too?" Holly asked.

"Me!" Gia and Patrick shouted again.

"That's a big, fat no, my friends," Maisy replied. "Mommy is not getting in any water that is not heated to at least eighty degrees."

Holly knew there would be no convincing her, but it was fun to try. It was nice to have some more family around for this holiday event. Their mom and dad were meeting them there as well. Holly felt like she needed a buffer between her and Jonah because something weird was happening.

She couldn't exactly explain it, but she knew that if she put herself in a position to be alone with him one more time, they were for sure going to end up making out. She could not make out with Jonah Drake again. It was nothing but a bad idea.

How did she know it was a bad idea? She wanted to do it so badly, that's how.

Maisy's husband, Danny, was in the driver's seat with a travel mug of coffee in his hand. "Did you bring a costume to wear this year?" he asked, backing out of the driveway.

When they did it as teenagers, Holly and Maisy both wore tutus over Christmas pajamas with their hair styled like Whos from Whoville. Last year, she had joined Randall and the rest of them as toy soldiers. This year, Holly wasn't as adventurous as she was industrious.

"I've got my Roadrunner T-shirt on under my jacket. I was hoping we could get a little free advertising while I freeze my booty off.

I also have knee-high Christmas socks that I'll pull over my leggings." She pulled them out of her bag to show her sister.

"Dad will love that. You're just like him. You are really good at marketing the bar. I just don't think like that."

"Well, someday when we run the Roadrunner, I'll handle the business side of things and you can run the kitchen."

"Good idea." Maisy glanced over her shoulder. "We'll make a good team."

"You know it," Holly replied with a wink.

When they arrived at the event, they pulled in next to Randall, Clarissa and Nancy. Randall had a bow tie around his neck and Clarissa was wearing a bridal veil.

"Gang's all here!" Randall clapped his hands together. "Are you guys ready to get loud? I need some loud cheerleaders when I run in that ice bath."

"Want to hear me scream?" Gia asked, hopping out of the van.

"Let's hear it."

Gia let out an eardrum-bursting screech. Randall held his hands over his ears. "Whoa! You might need to be careful. Noises like that start avalanches."

Gia had no idea what that meant but beamed with pride anyway. Holly noticed Jonah wasn't with them. Maybe he was coming on his own.

"I like your costume," Holly said to Clarissa.

"Thanks. We needed something last-minute and this is what Randall came up with. He said other people wear silly outfits. I didn't want to stand out too much."

"People wear some wild things. You'll see. It's all in good fun."

"There's our people!" Holly's mom and dad joined them in the parking lot. Her mom ran right for the kids. "My grandbabies."

Will noticed Clarissa's veil and frowned. "That's just a costume, right?" he whispered to Holly as she greeted him with a hug.

"It's just a costume. I don't think they're planning on eloping while they're here."

"Thank goodness."

People from Coyote and several of the surrounding small towns came to participate in the Frontier Freeze. Many came to cheer on their friends and family while the rest came to take the dip. There were groups of people in matching outfits, like the one dressed up as Santa's eight reindeer. There were families, couples and the single participants like Holly. People taking the plunge paid a fee for a spot in the Freeze. All the money raised was donated to a local children's hospital. It made the experience all that more worthwhile.

"Let's go check in," Randall said. "Howie, Old Red and Frank are waiting for us down by the water in the tent." He led the way to the check-in table.

Holly looked around for Jonah. She felt bad that they were all heading in without him but assumed that he would find them when he got here. She checked her phone to see if he had messaged her. The last text was from the night they sabotaged the wedding venue. The night they had kissed and they agreed they should not do that again.

Nothing since. She needed to remember that he wasn't required to check in with her. If he was coming, he could text his mom to find out where they were going to stand to watch the Freeze.

After checking in, the three of them found Uncle Howie, Frank and Old Red waiting in the heated participant tent. The three men were dressed like superheroes. They had either a mask, a cape or a trident. Uncle Howie carried around a speaker playing his character's theme song.

Coffee and hot chocolate were available to anyone taking the plunge to keep them warm on the inside as they prepared to shock their outside in the river. Holly used the time in the tent to put on her knee-high socks and the rubber boots she packed.

"You were right about the wild costumes," Clarissa said as she sipped her coffee. "I love the family of penguins over there." She nodded in their direction.

"Oh, the penguins are regulars. They dress up like that every year. I like that the Coyote volunteer fire department goes in with their full gear. I wonder if that stuff helps them stay warm in the cold like it protects them from burning up in a fire."

"Good question."

Holly couldn't resist asking about Jonah any longer. "Do you want me to text Jonah and let him know that everyone is already down by the river with the other spectators?"

"That's sweet, but he got an emergency call late last night and hadn't come home when we left. I honestly don't know if he's going to make it. He's got quite a bit of sleep to catch up on."

"Oh." The disappointment hit her like a ton of bricks.

"I know he was looking forward to coming. He kept giving me a hard time, saying he didn't believe that I was going to go through with it. I sure hope someone gets a picture of me, so I can prove to him that I did it."

Holly pulled out her phone and sent Maisy a text. "I'll make sure my sister takes a video. You will have all the proof you need."

"Thank you. I really do appreciate that you and Jonah have been so supportive. It's also because of you two that I feel like I've been getting to see inside Randall's world a little bit more. I don't think I would have gone to the rodeo if Jonah hadn't pushed me a bit just like I think I have you to thank for getting Randall to come to the gingerbread contest. He told me he didn't think he was going to have any fun, but now he plans to win every year."

Basically, she was saying everything Jonah and Holly had done to get them to see how incompatible they were had done the exact opposite. To top it off, spending all this time together had created this troublesome need to kiss Jonah again, which was only going to end badly. If her dad was against Uncle Randall marrying a Drake, he would never accept that his daughter wanted to date one.

"All right, do either of you lovely ladies need more coffee before we jump in the river?" Randall asked.

"I'm good," Holly said. Clarissa also declined.

The event organizers announced it was time to line up. Clarissa held Randall's hand, and Holly suddenly felt like a third wheel. It made her miss Jonah even more than she already did. They moved out of the tent and headed for the riverbank.

"They only let you go into the water that's no more than knee-deep," Randall explained to Clarissa. "Some people sit down and get themselves completely soaked, but you can just get in up to your knees."

"That's all I'm going to do," Holly said. "Trust me, that's wet enough."

"Come on, Hol," Frank said. "You can't wimp out and only run in and out. Neck-deep or it didn't happen." Her father's cousin loved to give her a hard time.

"You don't make the rules for me, Frank. If I want to go up to my knees, I'll go up to my knees."

"Nobody messes with Holly," Randall said to Clarissa. "She reminds me so much of my mom, her great-grandma. Tough as nails, smart as a whip and true blue."

"I can see that." Clarissa reached out and gave Holly's hand a squeeze.

The sun was out but the temperature was still hovering around freezing. Just after Thanksgiving, the area had eight inches of snow dumped on it and none of that had melted since then. The crowd of spectators stood all around the riverbank, split in the middle by the aisle that the participants would walk down and back. In the river stood five fully suited rescue workers in a semicircle. They had their dive suits on and their job was to make sure no one got caught in the river's current and went downstream.

It didn't take long for them to spot the Hayward crew in the crowd. They were, by far, the loudest people there. Holly found herself scanning the rest of the spectators, hoping that Jonah had shown up. Her heart sank when there was no sign of him.

Why was she letting this bother her so? Wasn't it better that he wasn't here? The more time they spent together, the more confused her feelings got. She didn't need this added complication in her life.

When they were just about to head to the water, she heard a voice coming from behind. "Excuse me. Sorry. Excuse me. I just need to catch up to my group. Sorry. Excuse me."

She turned around and there was Jonah dressed in a yellow tank top and purple basketball shorts with a sweatband around his head.

"Jonah!" Clarissa exclaimed with the same joyfulness Holly felt in her heart.

"What are you doing? What are you wearing?" Holly was trying to process if this was real or the cold was beginning to cloud her brain.

"Sorry I'm late. I didn't want to miss this and I realized I didn't want you to jump in the river alone, either. I'm not forfeiting."

"And you decided to wear that?" She could feel her smile widen.

"I figure the less wet clothes I have touching my body, the faster I will warm up when we get out, so I dressed as LeBron James. I got the headband and everything."

He was hilarious and adorable and that urge to kiss him was back a thousand times stronger than before. She was in big trouble.

Their group finally made it to the shoreline. The three superheroes went first, and Frank flopped in and then popped out of the water with his trident held high. The crowd went wild, and Holly knew that she had to fully submerge herself or she'd never hear the end of it. Plus, now that Jonah was here, she needed to up her game.

For a moment Holly thought Clarissa was going to back out, but Randall swept her up in his arms bridal style and walked them both in and out. Her feet never touched the water. It was ridiculously romantic and left Holly feeling guilty once again for wanting to break them up.

"You ready for this?" Jonah asked, standing at her side.

"More ready than you, I bet."

"Of course you are," he said with a laugh. He held out his hand and Holly stared at it for a second before taking hold. His touch sent a blast of heat through her body and she knew the water wasn't going to bother her one bit.

JONAH HAD NEVER felt anything as cold as the river during the Frontier Freeze. He was unsure how it was not ice at this temperature. The only thing keeping him from running back on shore was the woman holding his hand and the smile on her face.

"You going to go all the way, Dr. Drake?"

"All the way?"

They went in far enough that the water was almost to Holly's hips. She let go of him and put both arms out to her sides. She closed her eyes and fell backward into the icy river. When she resurfaced, her dark hair looked almost black against her pale skin. She rose out of the water and he could hear her whole family screaming for her in the crowd.

"You are kidding yourself if you think I'm going to do that," he said. "You're turning blue. You win. Let's get out of here."

He took her by the hand again and they ran out of that death pool of hypothermia.

Jonah was so cold that he could barely feel her hand in his, but he knew he didn't want to let go.

"Man, that was cold," she said with her teeth chattering.

Jonah pulled her closer and dropped her hand so he could wrap his arm around her and hold her against him. "I can't believe you did that. Let's get you in that heated tent and back into some dry clothes."

"I can't believe you made it. Your grandma said you had an emergency call last night. Aren't you beyond tired right now?"

"There's nothing like one-degree water to wake you up. I'm wide awake now."

"I'm glad you made it," she said, looking up at him like she meant it.

Jonah felt that tug. He wanted to cradle her wet face and kiss her slightly blue-tinted lips. When they had kissed the other night, he hadn't wanted it to end. But the look on her face when they came apart had made him realize that he couldn't push her or she was going to run.

"You did it!" Maisy appeared out of nowhere with a giant bath towel that she quickly wrapped around her sister.

The whole Hayward crowd had surrounded them. Jonah's mom was the sole Drake. She held out a towel for him. "I brought this for your grandmother, but I think you need it more than she does."

"Did you hear how loud everyone was when I came up out of the water?" Holly's cousin Frank asked.

"I love that Randall carried Clarissa in and kept her dry. That was very sweet of you," Maisy said.

Gran looked cold even though she wasn't wet. "I started to panic and he just lifted me right off my feet."

"That's how a groom is supposed to treat his bride, isn't it?" Randall gave her a kiss on the cheek.

"We should change out of these wet clothes," Holly said, still shivering from head to toe. "We'll meet you guys in the parking lot?"

"Breakfast at the Roadrunner in a half hour," Will said. "Mom and I are going to go set up. You guys meet us there once you're dry."

"You feel up to some breakfast?" Holly asked Jonah. "Or do you need to head back home to get some sleep? I totally get it if you need to go to bed, but you're also welcome to join us for breakfast. You probably didn't have time to eat before you came."

"I would love some breakfast."

Her rosy red cheeks were round like cherries as she smiled. "Okay, I'll meet you back out here after we change?"

"Sounds good."

There were three heated tents. One for refreshments and two for participants in the Freeze to change into dry clothes. Holly headed inside the women's tent.

"I can't believe you came and I can't believe you went in," his mom said as all the Haywards scattered.

"I didn't have anything better to do. And I thought the water would help me stay awake better than standing on the sidelines."

"Nothing better to do, huh?" She smirked and shook her head. "You are just as bad as your grandmother, you know. These Haywards have gotten under your skin."

"Is that bad?" His mother had been on board with him interfering with the wedding, but at the same time seemed to be fully supporting Gran with getting the wedding planned. She also got along well with Holly when they were all together. He knew she didn't carry the same grudges his father had.

"If you could see the look on your face whenever you are near her, you wouldn't have to ask me that question. I have been waiting to see that look in your eyes for years now."

Was he really that obvious? Given the way he had been feeling lately, probably. He wasn't going to deny it any longer. The only thing was would Holly feel the same?

There was only one way to find out. He ran to the changing tent and got out of his wet clothes and into his dry, warm ones. His decision to wear as little as possible turned out to be an excellent one because it did not take him long to feel almost normal again. He carried his wet clothes out in the kitchen garbage bag he had grabbed on his way out of the house.

His mom was standing outside the tent talking to Janet Williams and Gran. Jonah didn't see Holly or Randall yet.

"Wow, you got ready fast," his mom said as he joined them.

"The secret is don't wear a lot and you have less to change out of."

"Smart," Janet said. "You've always been so smart. I remember when you were in my biology class and you had to correct Mr. Bronson when he was trying to explain some complicated biology thing that the rest of the class had no clue about. But Jonah knew— he made the teacher look like an idiot. I remember laughing so hard."

Jonah forgot about that. He had corrected the teacher in front of the whole class. He had been so pretentious back then, acting like he was smarter than everyone when there was no way he had been. No wonder why Holly had hated him in high school.

"I was annoying."

"Oh, don't say that." Janet put a hand on his shoulder. "You were so funny in high school. Smart, funny, handsome. It's no wonder all the girls were in love with you back then."

"High school girls are easy to impress, I guess." Not all high school girls, of course. To impress someone like Holly, you really had to earn it. She didn't base things on superficial things like looks.

"I was telling your mom that our families should get together for the holidays. Maybe we could do New Year's together."

Out of the corner of his eye, Jonah spotted Holly. He caught a glimpse of her face before she whipped around and started marching up the hill to the parking lot. That was when he noticed Janet was still touching him.

He carefully extracted her hand from his body. "It was good to see you, Janet. We'll have to get back to you about New Year's. We have to go meet some friends for breakfast."

Friends. Was it possible the Drakes and the Haywards could be friends? Could they be more?

Randall came out of the changing tent and Jonah knew he needed to catch up to Holly. "Randall, you got my mom and gran?" When Randall nodded, Jonah took off. "I'll meet you guys at the Roadrunner."

He raced up the hill, carefully weaving his way through the crowd. He caught up to Holly as she was waving down her sister and brother-in-law as they were leaving. They stopped and put the minivan in Reverse.

Jonah could hear the Christmas music playing inside even before Danny rolled down his window.

"You guys okay?"

"Can you give us a second?" Jonah asked.

Holly spun around, unaware that he had been behind her.

"You said we were going to meet back up outside the tent."

The light in her eyes was gone. Her expression was as cold as that river they had just gotten out of. "You looked otherwise engaged. I figured if you wanted to eat, you'd meet us all over there. I get it if you have other plans."

Was she jealous? The possibility made him feel absolutely giddy. Feeling jealous meant she felt something for him. "I don't have other plans, Holly. I want to go to breakfast...with you."

She stared at him for a second and took a step back. "Then we'll meet you over there."

He didn't want her to get in that minivan. "You could drive with me. If you wanted to."

He watched as she contemplated her options. Her mind clearly whirling. "What would Janet Williams think?" she finally said, revealing where the cold shoulder was coming from.

He let himself enjoy her jealousy a second longer and then he ended her misery. "Hopefully, she will think I'm not as eligible as she wants me to be."

CHAPTER ELEVEN

HOLLY SLID INTO the passenger's seat and promptly put on her seat belt. She was quiet, but Jonah didn't mind because she had chosen to come with him instead of going with her sister. He turned the heat way up as soon as he started the truck.

"Let's get you warmed up as quickly as possible. Your lips were literally blue when you got out of the water. I was afraid you were going to turn into a block of ice."

"I'm fine. Once I got out of those wet clothes, I felt a million times better."

"I bet. I'm glad my gran didn't go in. I think the cold would have been a major shock to her system. Randall keeps proving himself to be a good guy."

"Yeah, well, your grandmother is way too nice. She has no idea how much she's torturing me by being so sweet every time we're together. I just need her to turn into a nasty bridezilla or something. If she was more like your aunt Stacy, I could stomach ruining their wedding a little better."

Jonah understood what she was feeling. It was the same thing keeping him up at night. "I feel like we started all this because we thought that the truth would reveal itself if we put them in these situations. But maybe the truth is that they belong together. Maybe we need to accept that they were right and we were wrong."

Holly let out a sardonic laugh. "Okay, you tell my dad that. If you can convince him, then I'll give up."

"Your dad and my uncle. I think it helped my uncle to know that they were planning to sign some kind of prenup to keep their finances separate, but I haven't had a chance to talk to him about it. Maybe he could come around and then your dad would, too."

"My dad is not coming around. You have to understand how deep his resentments run. I don't think the prenup is going to change his position on things in the slightest. He wants me to do whatever it takes to stop this wedding."

Jonah worried he was in that same boat

with Oliver. "Everyone else seems to be coming around. What would happen if Oliver and your dad ended up being the only holdouts? Would that be so bad?"

"I don't know," she said with a sigh. She turned her head and stared out the window. "Can we talk about something else? I don't want to be sad and talking about this hopeless situation makes me feel nothing but sad."

There were only two things on Jonah's mind lately. One was his grandmother's Christmas wedding and the other was the kiss he and Holly had shared. Something told him she didn't want to talk about that, either. "Why don't you tell me what you want for Christmas," he suggested.

She glanced back at him and he saw that little smile playing on her lips. "What? Did you just turn into Santa Claus all of a sudden? From LeBron to good ole Saint Nick?"

"Come on, curious minds want to know. What does Holly Hayward want for Christmas? You're kind of a mystery. I don't know what could be on this list of yours."

"I don't have a list. I haven't had a list in a very, very long time."

"Now, that's sad. Humor me. If you were to write a list because you could ask for anything at all, what would be on that list?"

"I can ask for anything?"

"Anything."

"Well, then, obviously, I would put an electric blue Jeep Wrangler Rubicon 392 on there because who wouldn't want the best four-wheeler SUV on the market?"

"Really? You're a Jeep girl, huh? I pictured you more of a pickup kind of person."

"Nope, I have always wanted a Wrangler. Could never afford one, but always wanted one. I would also put a Bartender in a Box on my list."

His interest was piqued. "What in the world is that?"

"You've never seen one? I read about it on this list of next year's hottest gadgets. It's this contraption that you fill up with the ingredients, and it basically mixes the perfect drink for you."

"But you're a bartender."

"Exactly! That's why I want one. It would be nice to come home and have someone or something make me a drink for once." He loved the way she thought about things.

"What about you, Dr. Drake? What does someone like you have on your Christmas list?"

Jonah was much like Holly. He didn't think too much about what he wanted for Christmas anymore. He enjoyed buying things for those he loved and he did his best to put smiles on their faces.

"I'm kind of a minimalist. I'm not into having a lot of things. Every year I ask for a bottle of my favorite whiskey and some new boots. Gran and Mom always come through."

"Whiskey, you say? What would your favorite whiskey be?"

"I am an Angel's Envy guy." He knew she'd know her whiskeys. He couldn't wait to hear what she thought of his choice.

Her bottom lip jutted out a bit as she nodded her head. "Angel's Envy. Interesting."

"Interesting good? Or interesting I have terrible taste in whiskey?"

"You have excellent taste in whiskey. I just pictured you more of a Four Roses guy."

"That would be my number two."

She had a disappointed frown. "I am usually spot-on when I guess someone's drink. I thought I had you pegged."

"You were close."

"You know I prefer winning over being close."

He might have made her frown, but she had this way of making him smile by just being her. "Oh, I know. It's beginning to be one of my favorite things about you."

They pulled into the parking lot of the Roadrunner and parked next to Danny and Maisy.

"You guys good?" Maisy asked Jonah after she unbuckled Gia from her booster seat.

Jonah gave her the thumbs-up and followed Holly into the Roadrunner. He should have been feeling more out of place than he did among all of these Haywards. He should have been looking for ways to show his grandmother that they didn't belong there, but that just wasn't how he felt at the moment.

Holly, Maisy and their mom got busy pushing some of the tables together to make one big table for them all to sit around. Randall made Gran a hot tea and swapped stories with Old Red about their favorite Frontier Freeze moments. Jonah's mom stood in front of the crooked Christmas tree with Danny. Both of them slowly cocked their heads to the side and then busted out laughing.

"Jonah, can you help Holly with the coffee?" Maisy asked. Holly scowled in her sister's direction, giving him the distinct impression that her sister was setting them up to go off somewhere alone much to her dismay.

"I would love to." He clapped his hands together. "Put me to work."

Holly pulled out a chair. "You literally worked all night. Why don't you sit and relax for five seconds? I can bring out coffee cups for everyone."

He refused, taking her by the hand and pulling her toward the bar. "I told you I am wide awake. Totally got my second wind. Let me help you."

She reluctantly showed him where they had a stash of coffee cups and he started placing them on a tray while she got a pot of coffee brewing.

"Do you serve a lot of coffee here on the regular?" he asked.

"I would say that the coffee is consumed by three people and three people alone in this town. Two of them are related to me and I am the third."

"I see. It's your work perk."

"Work perk? I like that. What's your work perk? Anyone ever send you home with something after delivering some baby goats or something?"

"I don't think I've ever gotten a work perk after delivering a goat. I do have one guy who gives me a Christmas ham every year to thank me for my work throughout the year. You ever had a farm-fresh ham before?"

"I don't think I have. Does it taste different than the kind my mom buys at the store?"

"I'm going to bring you a ham sandwich after Christmas and let you decide for yourself. I think it's pretty spectacular, but maybe I just forgot what store-bought hams taste like."

Holly leaned back against the bar. "Well, now I really want to try this ham."

"You know what I just thought of? What if we don't even have Christmas dinner this year? If we have a wedding, that sort of takes the place of anything we usually do on that day."

"How can they have a wedding if they don't have anywhere to have the wedding? I think there's a good chance there won't be a wedding this Christmas."

"She hasn't canceled yet," Jonah reminded her. "She was so upset when I told them that the Devonshire had backed out. I don't know what her plan B is yet, but Gran always has a plan B."

Holly stood tall. "I guess that means that it will be Randall who puts his foot down and says Christmas is off the table. That would mean I would win the bet."

Jonah picked up the tray of coffee mugs. "I am not going to give you the satisfaction of a response to that ridiculous claim."

"You just did," she retorted in a singsong voice.

He had to put some space between them, otherwise he was 99 percent sure that he was about to kiss that grin off her face.

HOLLY'S HEART WAS beating at close to a million beats per minute. When Jonah looked at her the way he did, she was sure she was going to combust. It was the same way he had looked at her before he kissed her outside the Devonshire. Something she had been replaying in her mind pretty much a thousand times a day since it happened.

She grabbed the coffeepot and carried it over to the table, offering to pour a cup for anyone who was interested. She tried her best to stop the heat from creeping up her neck and getting to her face.

Maisy and Bonnie got everyone plates and silverware, while their dad and Howie were in the kitchen cooking up some eggs, pancakes and sausage.

"Thank you, sweetheart," Randall said when Holly placed the hot cup of coffee in front of him. "There's nothing like hanging out together at the Roadrunner."

She placed a hand on his shoulder. "I know."

Holly loved when her whole family gathered together at the bar for a meal like this. It didn't even bother her that there were three Drakes in the mix. Holly glanced over at Jonah. Was it possible they could all get along and spend more days like this together?

"So how did things go at the Devonshire the other day?" Yvonne asked Randall and Clarissa.

"It was beautiful," Clarissa said. "But they said that they couldn't accommodate us. The woman over there wasted our time, giving us a tour and selling us on all they could do, then called Jonah and told us they couldn't do any of it on Christmas."

"They couldn't do it *this* Christmas," Jonah said, even though he knew full well that there was no way Megan would ever offer up that space to the Haywards.

"Regardless, we've decided to get married on the ranch," Randall said. "They have a heated barn where we could have the ceremony."

Holly felt like a balloon that had been floating toward the clouds only to pop, causing it to fall back to earth. They weren't postponing. They had found their plan B. There was no one who could stop them from having the wedding on Clarissa's property.

"That's a safe alternative. You won't have

to worry about anyone canceling on you," Old Red said.

"Are you planning the reception there as well?" Holly's mom asked.

Randall and Clarissa exchanged looks. Randall cleared his throat. "Actually, we were hoping that we could have the reception here at the Roadrunner."

There was one person who would stop them from having the reception at the Roadrunner, though.

"What do you think, Bonnie? Do you think that William will give us the green light to have the party here?"

Since Holly's mom had no idea how he truly felt about this wedding, she had no qualms about screaming yes. "We would absolutely love to host your reception. You're family, Randall. We'll do whatever it takes to help out family."

"Breakfast is served," Dad said, coming out of the kitchen with platters of pancakes and sausage in his hands. Howie was right behind him with an oversize stainless steel bowl full of scrambled eggs.

"Smells amazing, Dad," Holly said.

"Tastes even better," Danny said, snatching a sausage link right off the platter and taking a bite.

"Will, Randall needs our help," Bonnie said. "He's decided to get married on Clarissa's ranch and was wondering if we could host a reception here. Isn't that a great idea?"

Will's grin wiped away instantly. He set the platters of pancakes down and stroked his long beard. "I'm sorry. For a second there I thought you said that Randall was going to have his reception here at the Roadrunner."

"That's what I said. We could handle that, don't you think? We're not open on Christmas Day. It wouldn't be hard to do."

The last thing Will wanted was to be open on Christmas Day so he could host a wedding reception for two people he had been praying would break up since he found out they were together. "You want to have the reception here?" he asked Randall specifically.

"We'd be awfully grateful if we could have it here. With such short notice, finding somewhere to host the party has proven to be more challenging than we expected. We thought about doing everything on the ranch, but we'd have to rent tables and chairs. The Roadrunner already has everything we need to host a dinner and drinks. You even have a dance floor."

Holding her breath, Holly prayed her dad didn't say something he would regret. He was taking his time to answer, which was good. Her mom preached to him all the time about thinking before he spoke. Other than the little kids, the rest of the family seemed equally anxious about how Will was going to respond. Maisy was biting her thumbnail. Frank, who was on Team Stop the Wedding, looked like he was watching the horse he bet on go neck and neck to the finish line with a horse owned by Oliver Drake. He was mouthing no and shaking his head ever so slightly.

"Seems to me that maybe a higher power is trying to tell you that you shouldn't be trying to have this wedding so soon after you got engaged," her dad eventually said. "Maybe you should think about postponing until you can have the wedding you really want in the place you really want to have it."

Holly made eye contact with Jonah before checking Randall's reaction to that suggestion. This was the newest goal.

"Like I've said before, we're not postponing. If we have to go to the courthouse and get married without any of the fanfare, that's what we'll do. We were just hoping the people we love would want to be included in our day."

The room went silent as all eyes were on Will. "Fine," he said, quickly retreating to the kitchen. "Frank, Holly, come help me."

It was pretty obvious to Holly why he needed her and Frank. She set the coffeepot down on the table as the rest of the family dug into the food. As soon as she and Frank stepped in the back, her dad confessed to feeling quite differently than he presented out there.

"I am not throwing them a wedding reception. I can't do it."

"Thank goodness," Frank said in relief.

"You just told them you would," Holly reminded them.

Will wiped his hands and threw the hand towel over his shoulder. "We are going to stop this wedding before it can happen. We're going to make sure I don't have to host a reception."

"I've been trying. I have done everything

I can to make them second-guess themselves or at the very least consider postponing. Nothing is working."

"We need to forget about getting them to reconsider," Frank said. "We need them to break up."

"We need to figure out what's a deal breaker for Randall and then set it up," Will said.

Holly was so tired. They had come to the point in this conflict where it was time to admit defeat. "They love each other, you guys. I know we were told not to trust a Drake, but Randall loves her."

"Pfft! They haven't known each other long enough to be in love," Will said, tossing some dirty dishes into the sink.

This from the man who had told his friend he was going to marry her mom the night he met her. Holly didn't know how long it took to fall in love. She had thought she was in love a couple of times and neither relationship worked out, so she didn't feel experienced enough to judge.

"Well, I don't know what would be a deal breaker for Randall."

"I'll figure it out," Frank said. "You need

to promise us that you'll help make it happen."

"We can do this." Will handed Holly two bottles of syrup. "Promise me you're still with us."

Was she? He wouldn't be asking her if he knew she had kissed Jonah the other day and liked it. In a flash, she felt guilty for being what her dad would see as disloyal. Family was everything to her.

"I'm with you. If you two can think of something, I'll do my best to see it through."

The two men nodded and they rejoined the breakfast. Holly took her seat in between her sister and Jonah. Everyone ate and laughed. The conversations were lively. It didn't matter what their last name was, everyone got along. Holly couldn't help but think that maybe it wasn't Randall and Clarissa who needed to have a change of heart. Maybe she should be hoping her dad and his cousin would.

Jonah was kind enough to help clear the table when the meal was over. He even offered to wash dishes.

"You don't have to do that. You should head home and get some sleep."

"Trying to get rid of me, huh?"

"Trust me, if I wanted to get rid of you, you'd be gone."

One corner of his mouth lifted as he chuckled. "No doubt."

They both reached for the same coffee mug and their hands touched. Holly felt that familiar jolt of electricity. She pulled her hand away not because she didn't want to be near him but because of the exact opposite.

"I was really glad you came today. It wouldn't have been as fun without you," she said. "But my dad will never let you step foot in the Roadrunner again if he catches you and me getting too cozy back here."

Jonah pushed his messy brown hair back and laughed. "Time for me to go home, huh?"

"I think so."

Jonah peeked out into the bar. Satisfied that they had a few moments of privacy, he reached for her hand. "Before I go, I want you to know that I was really glad I came today, too. I've been thinking about what happened on Tuesday and I wanted to make sure that you don't hate me for giving in to these feelings that I've been having."

"I don't hate you."

He interlaced their fingers. "I don't hate you, either."

"Look at us finding more things we have in common."

His head bobbed with quiet laughter. "We are getting better at that. What if we tried to do something together that didn't have anything to do with this wedding or our families' feud to see if we can find a couple other things we have in common?"

"Like a date?" Holly's stomach did a flip. It made her excited and terrified at the same time.

"We don't have to call it a date if that makes you want to say no," he offered.

It was totally a date, but he was right, not calling it that made it easier for her to agree to the madness. "I might be willing to go on a hike with someone around Raven Lake tomorrow morning. Are you free?"

"I think I am. Should I pick you up at ten?"

"Since it's not a date, I think we should meet there."

"Hey, Holly—" Maisy came through the swinging door. Holly and Jonah jumped apart, which probably made what they were doing look more suspicious than it was. "Oh, sorry. I didn't mean to—"

"What? You didn't do anything. Nothing is happening." Which was something someone said when something was absolutely happening. "What did you need?"

"I was going to ask about something, but it can wait."

Jonah pointed at the door behind Maisy. "You stay. I was just leaving." Another thing that people said when they were caught doing things they shouldn't.

Maisy pressed her lips together. She didn't buy anything they were selling, but moved farther into the kitchen so he could get past her.

"Thanks again for breakfast. I'll see you later. Both of you. Or one of you at a time. Like around town or at the wedding. Whatever. Who knows, right?"

Jonah would be the last person on earth that Holly would ever want to cover for her because he was absolutely terrible at playing it cool.

As soon as he was gone, Maisy was in stitches. Holly went back to the dishes, pretending in vain that nothing had happened.

"I knew you and Uncle Randall were a lot alike, but man, Holly, this is wild. I cannot wait to see how this plays out."

Deep down, Holly couldn't, either.

CHAPTER TWELVE

THE RAVEN LAKE TRAIL was a fairly easy two-mile out-and-back hike. The views of the Rocky Mountains were incredible and Raven Lake was one of the most beautiful lakes in all of Colorado with its crystal-clear water. It wasn't unheard of to be able to see fish swimming near the water's edge. Jonah and some friends used to snowshoe this area when he was younger.

It had snowed the night before, covering everything in the freshest white fluff. It crunched under his feet. Holly was dressed in layers, ready for the cold weather. She had on her big black hiking boots, jeans, a fleece sweatshirt and a puffy red vest. Her red-and-white-striped stocking hat had a huge pom-pom on top.

"Of course, it had to snow right before we go hiking," she said, slipping her arm through the strap of her backpack. "We should have brought snowshoes."

"I was just thinking that!" Somehow, they had gone from being complete opposites to in sync. "I used to come out here with the Thompson brothers and snowshoe all the time."

"Maisy and I snowshoe this trail at least once a month in the winter. We hike it once a week in the spring and the summer. The wildflowers are absolutely my favorite thing about this trail."

Jonah loved that. He knew exactly where he was going to take her the next time they got together for a nondate. "So, you snowshoe but don't ice-skate. What about skiing? Do you ski?"

"Skiing is a rich man's sport, my friend. I did go to Breckenridge with some friends when I turned twenty-one. They paid for my lift ticket and my ski rental as my birthday gift. It was the only way I was getting on those mountains."

"Did you like it?"

"I was totally intimidated at first, and I didn't want to admit that I had no clue what I was doing. That meant there were no warm-up runs on the bunny hill. I got on that ski lift and went for it right away."

"And how did that end?"

"Not well. I took out a small child, two women and a group of teenage boys when I finally crashed after flying down the slope at about three hundred miles a minute because I had no idea how to slow myself down."

Jonah's eyes widened. "Sounds like you needed a friend to do a little coaching. I bet you would have figured it out real quick with some help."

"I got better by the end of the weekend, but I haven't gone back since."

He added another nondate activity for them to try to his mental list.

"What about you? Do you ski?" she asked.

"I love skiing, but it's been hard to fit in trips to the mountains with work. My gran wasn't exaggerating about my lack of work-life balance. I really enjoy it, though. I like being outside in the fresh air. I think that's why I chose to be a large animal vet versus a guy in an office all day. I needed to be outside."

They came up on the first big curve in

the trail. "What made you want to be a vet in general?"

"Living on the ranch for sure," he answered without hesitation. "I don't think I appreciated how much went on at the ranch when I was younger and we would only visit for a week or so at a time. Living there opened my eyes to a whole other world. I got to spend more time with the animals, help take care of them. Then, one night at three a.m., I got to see one of the horses give birth and I fell in love with being part of the process, part of...life. Does that sound weird?"

"No, not at all. That's kind of how I feel about working at the Roadrunner." Jonah assumed she was being sarcastic, but she was quick to clarify. "Now, hear me out because I know serving food and drinks to humans is not the same thing as helping bring a baby horse into the world, but I did realize at an early age that I needed to be around people. When I'm at the Roadrunner, I am surrounded by new and familiar faces. I love being part of the banter and listening to other people's stories. I feel like I have a purpose."

It was what everyone was looking for in

life—a reason to get up every day. Jonah found it working with animals and Holly found it behind the bar at the Roadrunner.

"Who needs balance when you're doing something that you love?" Jonah asked.

"Right? Everyone needs to back off of us. I don't know why people think you have to get married and have kids to have a life."

"You don't want to get married and have kids?" He had never been against the idea, the right person simply hadn't come along yet, but he wondered if they had that in common as well.

Holly bent over and picked up some snow, patting it into a ball with her mitten-clad hands. "I wouldn't say I don't want to get married and have kids. I just don't feel like I have to."

"Same." Jonah picked up some snow as well because he didn't want to be unarmed in case this turned into a snowball fight. It was the best packing snow. Knowing Holly, anything was possible.

"I used to think it wouldn't be a big deal if I didn't do any of it because Randall was living his best life without ever getting married or having kids. Of course, he's decided that wasn't the way he wanted to leave this world. Now, I don't know if I have to reconsider all of my thoughts on the matter or not."

"I imagine my life with kids," Jonah admitted. "When I try to picture myself in the future, I see myself as a dad. I would love to teach my son or daughter about the ranch, about animals. I want to read books to them and help them with their math homework."

Holly smirked. "Of course you do." She dropped her snowball into the snow and began to roll it into the open field on their left. No snowball fight. She wanted to build a snowman. "I have a feeling that I would need my kids to teach me math. That wasn't my favorite subject. Besides the basics of addition, subtraction, multiplication and division, everything else in math is pointless. How many times in your life have you had to find the tangent of a triangle?"

Jonah put his snowball down and began to roll it into a bigger ball. "Never."

"Exactly, but we spent a whole year in geometry. Makes no sense."

"What was your favorite class in school?"

"Lunch?" she replied like it was a question instead of an answer.

"Lunch is not a class."

"Fine. What about PE? That's a class. We got grades and I usually got an A in that one."

"I will accept that as an answer. Can you guess what my favorite class was?"

Her snowball was huge and perfect for the base of a snowman. He rolled his over to it and picked it up to put on top. Holly tilted her head to one side and then the other. "It's not straight. Can you move it a little bit to the right?"

Jonah readjusted the snowman's upper torso. "Better?"

"Perfect," she said, giving him the thumbs-up and beginning the next snowball for the head. "I am going to guess your favorite was some kind of science class. Biology or chemistry. Something you use all the time in your job now."

She thought she had it all figured out. Jonah packed some snow into the gaps between the two snowballs. "Mr. Timmons's world history class."

"Oh my gosh!" Holly picked up the snowman's head and walked it over. "I loved Mr. Timmons! Remember when he used to dress up like a gladiator?"

"My favorite was when he used to make up raps at the beginning of each unit to give us a preview of what was coming up."

She placed the head on the snowman. "His rapping was epic. When he did the one about Mesopotamia to Snoop Dogg, I was hooked."

"Again, something we have in common."

"I never would have thought you and I could have ever agreed about anything school-related. You surprise me, Dr. Drake."

"I'm going to get some sticks for arms," he said, motioning toward the line of trees about a hundred yards away.

"Can you look for some pine cones for the eyes, too?" she asked as she carved a smile into the head.

Jonah went searching at the tree line for some fallen branches and pine cones. He found what he needed and an acorn cap that he thought would work well for a nose. With his hands full of snowman accessories, he headed back to the snowman and Holly.

That was the moment he realized he had

been lulled into complacency. While he was scavenging the tree line, she had stockpiled a large supply of snowballs and promptly began pelting him with them.

He dropped his snowman parts and as quick as he could hand-packed some snow-balls of his own. Holly had extraordinary aim. She could have been a Major League Baseball pitcher with that accuracy. Jonah took more than one smack in the middle of his chest and one on the head. She was ruth-less and he was pretty sure he had met his soul mate.

JONAH WAS AN easy target. Too easy. Holly was enjoying her direct hits more than she probably should. She had planned it out perfectly. He had no idea she was about to attack. Not only was she able to build her arsenal, she had the snowman shield while he was out in the wide open.

"You are such a sneak!" he shouted, dodg-ing one of her snowballs.

"I can't help it that you're too trusting." Holly ducked behind her snowman, who took a hit right to the head.

He was advancing on her with a big smile

on his face. "I thought we were friends, but now I know I can never turn my back on you. You are nothing but trouble."

She threw three back-to-back to keep him at bay. Jonah would not be deterred. He rushed at her and before she knew it, he was on top of her. He picked her up and carried her away from what was left of her snowballs.

When he put her down he was out of breath and so was she. It was like they were right outside the Devonshire again. This attraction was undeniable, even though it was unrealistic to think they could see this through. His hands left her waist and held her face. This time it was Holly who initiated the kiss. His lips were cold, but it didn't take long for them to heat up.

Before he pulled away, he brushed his nose against hers. "Sorry," he whispered.

"You don't have to apologize. I kissed you, remember?" Maybe she wasn't the only one disoriented by what was happening.

"Not for the kiss," he said, taking a step back.

Holly's brows drew together. If not for the kiss, then what?

Before she caught on, Jonah ran back to her snowballs and began to pelt her with her own weapons. She'd been beaten by the oldest trick in the book. The kissing distraction was a classic distraction technique.

"Stop." She held her hands up in defeat. "I surrender. You win."

He held the last snowball in his hand. "How can I believe you?"

"I'm a woman of my word. I want to finish the snowman."

He considered it for a second and tossed the snowball in the other direction. "Truce."

Holly walked over to where he had dropped the sticks and pine cones for the snowman and brought them back to him. "You have to admit, that was an amazing setup up on my part."

"I thought for sure you were going to throw that first snowball at me when we were walking. When you started making it a snowman, I completely dropped my guard. You got me good."

Jonah was so much more easygoing than she remembered him being when they were younger. He made her question her own memories. The more time they spent together, the more difficult it was to believe that he had ever been rude to her. In fact, she appreciated how understanding he was all the time.

They gave the snowman arms and eyes and Jonah stole her hat to finish him off. Holly made him pose for a picture with their new friend before stealing her hat back and returning to the trail.

Holly loved the Raven Lake Trail and, this time of year, it made her feel like she lived in some kind of winter wonderland. The snow-capped mountains were breathtaking. The frozen lake looked like glass.

Jonah told her about the pregnant horse they had at the ranch right now. He thought there might be a newborn foal by Christmas. Their conversation was easy and light-hearted. As they made their way around the lake, things shifted.

"I know we both chose not to talk about the kiss outside the Devonshire, but I'm wondering if we're going to talk about the one during the snowball fight," Jonah said.

Holly had always been a big fan of not talking about the things she knew weren't going to end well. "What if we just kept not talking about it?"

"If we decided that we wanted to do more of that kind of thing, I'm going to need to have a conversation about it."

"You want me to be mature and take responsibility for my actions? Is that what you're telling me, Jonah?"

"That's exactly what I'm asking you to do."

Being honest would be so much easier if there weren't so many outside factors making this relationship so complicated. Did Holly like Jonah? Yes. Did she want to keep kissing him? Absolutely. If she liked him and wanted to kiss him, would her father lose his mind? For sure.

"If I admit I like you, then I also have to admit that this thing between us is doomed. Part of me wants to keep living in this weird limbo where we don't acknowledge that we have these feelings for each other, but we still get to kiss."

Jonah took that in for a moment. His expression was dulled. "And there's no chance that at some point in the future you could see this thing working out. That it could be something real that happens in the world."

"If by 'in the world' you mean in front of my dad, that would be a solid no."

A sadness clouded his features. "Well, then we have to stop whatever this thing is now."

Holly hated to make him feel bad, especially since up until this point their time together had been everything she could have hoped it would be. She wasn't going to lie to him, though.

"You understand our families' history, right? That my great-grandfather worked on your family's ranch back in the 1930s?"

"I don't know all the details, but yes, I know he worked on the ranch."

"He didn't just work there, he was the ranch manager. He was your great-great-grandfather's right-hand man. At the tail end of the Depression and the beginning of World War II, everyone was struggling. Your family needed my great-grandfather to help them run the ranch, but there wasn't enough money to pay him. To convince him to stay on, an offer of a lifetime was made. Your family didn't have cash on hand, but one thing they did have that many others did not was land. I'm sure you know that back then, your family was the biggest landowner in Coyote."

"I know all this, Holly. I know that there was a dispute over some land. I don't know what it has to do with us."

"Your family promised my great-grandfather a piece of land just north of your ranch. No one disputes that. That land had the potential to change things for my family. It was going to mean financial independence and room to raise their families."

"But then our great-grandfathers went off to war," Jonah said, clearly frustrated. "They fought in the war and when they came back, some things had changed."

"Your great-great-grandfather had died while they were gone. That was the only thing that had changed. He was the one who had made the deal with my great-grandfather. Yours took advantage of the fact that there was nothing in writing and took the land away."

"To take care of his family, my great-grandfather had to make some tough choices and one of them was to sell the land to some-one else."

"According to my family, it was more personal than that. He reneged on his dad's promise. He sold the land out from under my great-grandfather even though he had earned it."

"According to my family, he gave your great-grandfather some money. He did his best to settle the debt. Maybe not the way your great-grandfather wanted him to, but it was the way that made the most sense for his family. My family."

His version of the story made it sound like there was just a change in payment, but the truth was the land was way more valuable than the money that was paid out. Holly's great-grandfather had also started making plans for that land he had been promised. He spent money on things because he be-lieved he was going to own that land. When he didn't own it, there was no getting any of that money back. The money Jonah's great-grandfather paid had to go toward those debts.

"I don't think you understand the ripple effects of that decision. Obviously, after he had been wronged, my great-grandfather couldn't go back to work for your family. So, not only did he not have his own land that he had planned on, he had no job. It changed everything for my family."

Jonah's eyes were full of remorse. "I can't change what someone in my family did eighty years ago, Holly. I won't sit here and defend what he did, but none of us know what was going on and why he did what he did for sure. None of those people are alive to explain or make it right."

"I'm not asking you to make it right. I'm trying to explain why the resentments run so deep. After that, your family didn't just survive, they *thrived* and mine suffered. Those differences and the reasons for them colored all Drake/Hayward interactions moving forward. Our grandparents did not get along. Our parents did not get along. We did not get along."

"I wanted to get along with you. I still want to get along with you."

"Certain family members, like my dad, can't let it go."

"Your dad can't let it go or *you* can't let it go?"

Not too long ago, she would have lumped herself in that category as well. Since spending time with Jonah, she'd been more torn. It wasn't fair to hold him responsible for something that wasn't his fault.

"I'm trying to."

"But you're not there yet and you don't know if you'll ever get there." Jonah sounded dejected. He let out a sigh. "That's all I needed to know."

Holly didn't mean to ruin the mood. This was the reason she didn't want to have this conversation in the first place. She couldn't lie about how she was feeling. She also didn't blame him for being a bit peeved. She was mad at herself for being the reason she couldn't enjoy something good like meeting a man who made her happy. When would she get out of her own way?

CHAPTER THIRTEEN

"HAVE YOU ORDERED the champagne?" Randall asked. "I want a bottle on every table."

Holly refilled the napkin dispenser. "You hovered over my shoulder while I was entering the order into the computer."

"Yeah, but I didn't see you complete the sale. And you're always doing ten things at once around here. Something could slip through the cracks and I don't want it to be my wedding champagne."

There didn't seem much reason to sabotage this wedding anymore. Her dad still hadn't come up with this terrible thing they could exploit that would be a deal breaker for Randall.

"I ordered your champagne. You gave me your credit card, remember?"

"I remember. I'm going to be checking that statement with a fine-toothed comb. I don't want to see any unusual purchases on there, missy."

Holly rested a hand on her hip. "You ask me for all this help, but won't let me buy myself something nice?"

He drummed his fingers on the counter and seemed to be attempting to tell if she was kidding or not. "You know that I'll buy you anything you need."

"Thank you, but I don't need anything, Uncle Randall. You don't have to worry about me using your card for anything other than all of the necessities for the reception like the champagne."

"What about the tablecloths?"

"Got 'em."

"And those candles we looked at?"

"On their way. We got two-day shipping."

"You're the best, Hol. I knew I could count on you."

She hoped he never found out what she had done to try to ruin the day for him. Uncle Randall only wanted to be happy, and Clarissa made him happier than he had ever been. That much was obvious.

He slid off his barstool. "I'm going to pick

you up tonight at ten to seven. We don't want to be late."

Holly's forehead puckered. "Late for what?"

"The toy drive wrapping thing that the people at Clarissa's church are doing tonight. You're the one who told me I needed to go. When you tell me to go, it always means you're coming with me."

She forgot about the present-wrapping party. It had been two days since Holly left Jonah in the parking lot after their hike. After she told him that she wasn't capable of letting the past go or taking that risk to be honest about how she felt about him to her dad. They hadn't spoken or texted since.

"I'm sure Jonah's going to be there. You two always find a way to make everything we do fun. If you're worried about it being kind of boring like I am, do like I do, and remember that your person will be there."

"You think Jonah is my person?"

Randall's bushy gray eyebrows arched. "You don't?" He didn't wait for an answer. He headed for the door. "I'll see you at ten to seven. Be ready to go."

Holly picked up a glass and started wiping it down with a clean dish towel. How could Jonah be her person? They couldn't even manage to be friends. She ruined everything with her stubbornness.

"Where's Randall?" Will came bursting through the swinging kitchen door.

"He left. He's going to be back tonight. He and I are going to some present-wrapping event at Clarissa's church."

"You don't need to do that stuff anymore. It's kind of unlikely that she's going to do something that would be a deal breaker at a wrapping party. Man, that woman is some kind of saint, isn't she? Doesn't she do anything selfish or aggravating?"

She didn't. Clarissa Drake was thoughtful, kind and even a little bit funny when she wanted to be. She was very much like her grandson.

"Sorry, Dad. Not everyone with the last name Drake is a bad person."

Will wagged a finger at her. "Don't let them fool you, honey. They're good at making you think they're decent people who treat others fairly. You can't trust anyone with the last name Drake. My grandpa had to learn the hard way."

It was the same excuse over and over. His

grandfather had been wronged by them and they would be too if they put their faith in a Drake. Holly had believed that for thirty years, but now, she wasn't so sure.

"I can let Randall know you want to talk to him before we leave for the church," she offered.

"Thank you. I have a story for him." Will went back in the kitchen, leaving Holly to shine up the rest of the glasses that had come out of the dishwasher.

Maisy got to the Roadrunner just before Randall was set to pick Holly up. She came behind the bar with a lopsided grin.

"How's your day going, my dear sister?" She tied her apron around her waist.

"Fine. How is your day going?" Holly asked, feeling suspicious.

"It was good," she replied in a singsongy voice.

"I get the feeling you want me to ask you why it was good. Do you want to tell me why it was good?"

"Danny and I got some good news today."

Holly waited for her sister to spill the beans. After a couple of seconds, her patience waned. "And?"

Maisy beamed. "We were going to wait until we were all together on Christmas, but you know me, I can't keep a secret. We're pregnant!"

Holly didn't know they were trying. She thought their family had been complete. "Congratulations!"

The two sisters hugged. When Maisy pulled back, her eyes were damp with happy tears. "I've actually wanted another baby since Patrick turned two. I was beginning to think it wasn't going to happen and then I was late so I took a test this morning and it was positive!"

Holly helped her wipe her tears. "Oh, honey, I'm so happy for you. You are the best mom. This baby is so lucky."

"Don't tell Mom and Dad yet. Maybe telling you got it out of my system and I can keep it a secret until Danny and I are both there to tell them."

Their dad came out of the kitchen. "Randall?"

"Not here yet, Dad. I told you I would let him know you want to talk to him."

"Hi, Dad," Maisy said.

"Hey, Mais. Make sure to push the special tonight. I bought too much."

"I'm pregnant," Maisy blurted out.

"So much for keeping that secret," Holly said with a chuckle.

Their dad wrapped his arms around his baby girl. "Don't tell Mom yet. Danny really wanted to be there when I told you guys."

Holly knew there was only one way that wasn't happening. "Let's hope Mom doesn't show up here tonight."

Randall walked through the door and headed right for the bar. "I thought I better eat something before we go. Can I get a burger and fries?"

"I'm pregnant," Maisy announced for the third time. Holly shook her head.

"Congratulations!" Randall said. "Gia and Parker must be excited."

"Patrick," Holly corrected him.

"That's what I said. Gia and Patrick must be so excited."

"I think you better do a three-way call with Danny and Mom, Maisy," Holly suggested. "Otherwise the rest of the town is going to find out before she does and she's going to be mad."

Maisy winced. "You're probably right. I'll put your burger in, Randall. Dad, can I use your office for a second?"

"Go ahead. I need to talk to Randall anyway." Will walked around the bar and took a seat next to his uncle. "So I was talking to Frank today and he was telling me how he did a job for George Landry and not only did he refuse to pay what Frank was owed, he left a bad review on the internet. Frank called him up to confront him man-to-man instead of responding publicly over the internet. And George had the audacity to say that even though Frank fixed his plumbing issue, he felt he charged too much."

"Did Frank go way over the estimate?"

Will shook his head. "Nope. Estimate was right on the money and George still stiffed him and wrote a bad review."

"That man is dead to me, then. You don't bad-mouth my family like that and think I'm just going to sit by and let that go."

"That's what I said," Will said.

Holly couldn't help but interject. "Frank should respond to his review with his side of the story. People will read it and if he has other good reviews, they should believe his rebuttal to one bad one."

"I'll tell him that."

"I would have given George a lot of business now that I have the cash to spend," Randall said. "He really blew it for himself."

"I'm glad you're on our side about it," Will said, getting up off the stool.

"Of course, you're family. Like I said, no one gets to bad-mouth my family and get away with it."

"I'll let Frank know you've got his back." Will went in the back and Holly poured Randall his favorite drink.

"You don't think I'll have to wrap gifts tonight if I bring gifts. Don't you think it's acceptable to only bring the gifts?" he asked.

"I'm sure that if you inform them you have never wrapped a gift before, they won't let you wrap gifts. You can just help sort or something."

"Don't tell Clarissa I've never wrapped a present. I don't want her to think I don't give gifts."

"I've got your back, Uncle Randall."

Maisy came out of the kitchen with Randall's burger and fries. Once he was done eating, he and Holly left for the church. Holly did a double take when they got to his truck.

"What did you do?"

"I'm bringing some gifts."

His truck looked like an overstuffed version of Santa's sleigh. He had a red tarp covering an enormous mound of gifts in the back. Holly figured it was going to take them all night just to unload Randall's donation.

The whole basement of the Coyote Community Church was already filled with toys and other gifts sorted by age and gender. They came inside to see if there was something they could use to bring in all the toys Randall brought.

Jonah was standing by the door with a clipboard. Holly wasn't sure he was going to be there and her heart did an extra thump at the sight of him.

"Hey, we need a little help bringing in some donations. Do they have a cart or something we can use?" she asked him, thankful for something neutral to say to start their conversation.

"Um, yeah, let me ask my grandma."

He didn't seem very happy to see her. He probably expected her not to come. He had probably hoped she wouldn't. She missed that smile he usually wore.

JONAH HAD TO get his heart rate back to normal. He hadn't expected Holly to show up tonight, and wasn't sure if he should be happy or disappointed about it. His racing heart told him he was anxious about it at the very least.

He retrieved a cart and went outside with Holly to help her bring in what Randall wanted to donate. His eyes widened as they approached the truck.

"Did he buy out an entire toy store?"

"I think he might have," Holly answered. "We need like ten more carts."

Jonah figured Randall was trying to impress Gran once again. It was going to work, too. They started loading the first cart. It didn't take ten trips, but it took more than a few. They spent the next half hour sorting them into the different age groups. Thankfully, he had bought a bunch of video game consoles and fancy dolls.

"What should we do next?" Randall asked.

"We have different jobs. You can be a shopper or you can be a wrapper."

"Shopper," Randall said, raising his hand.

"I can wrap, I guess," Holly said. That was good because he was going to shop and if she wrapped, they wouldn't have to spend too much time together. He couldn't handle spending too much time together. Not when he knew she would never accept that it was better to leave the past in the past.

Clarissa took Holly over to the wrapping station while Jonah set Randall up with a family to shop for. All he had to do was reference his list for the age of the boys or the girls and then go to the appropriate area and pick three presents for each kiddo. Sometimes the list gave suggestions based on the child's preferences. Then he could take his list and his gifts over to the wrapping tables and pass them off to the wrappers who wrapped everything up in pretty paper and bows.

Jonah and Randall shopped one together so he made sure he understood how it worked. When they finished, they brought the gifts over to Clarissa.

Gran's whole face lit up. Every time she

was around Randall, she looked happier than he'd ever seen her. "Thank you, my dear."

"Make them pretty like you, sweetheart."

Jonah tried not to roll his eyes and went to get two more lists to shop. He gave Randall the one with fewer kids. They went off to shop, but Jonah's eyes kept falling back on the wrapping table where Holly was working.

She must have come straight from the Roadrunner because she had on a Roadrunner T-shirt and her hair was up in a ponytail. It didn't matter what she wore or how she did her hair, there was an effortless beauty about her. When she smiled, everyone around her smiled.

Greg Harmon was smiling and lingering at the wrapping table a little longer than he needed to. He and Holly ran in the same crowd in high school. Greg was recently divorced or so he announced when he said hello to Jonah earlier that evening. Holly laughed at something he said and the two of them high-fived.

Jonah was green with envy. He tried to refocus on his shopping list. He had an eight-year-old girl, a five-year-old boy and a two-year-old boy. He finished the girl and moved on to the boy section.

Greg was still at the wrapping table. Didn't he know he was supposed to drop off the gifts and go get another list to shop? He wasn't supposed to stand there and distract the wrappers from getting their wrapping done. It was going to slow down the whole process. Not to mention Holly was still smiling and laughing at whatever he was saying and Jonah was beginning to feel red with anger.

From green to red. At least his emotions were festive for the holiday. He finished the boys and brought his gifts up to the wrapping table. Holly was done with Greg's gifts, but he hadn't moved on. Jonah placed his gifts in front of her.

"You're ready for a new family? Or does Greg have some more gifts to be wrapped?"

"Oh, I'm done. I should probably get some more, huh? Holly was distracting me from my work. It was nice catching up."

"Yeah, good to see you, Greg." Holly smiled brightly.

"I'll be back," Greg said with a wink.

Jonah's stomach turned. He placed the

rest of his gifts in front of her and handed her the list. "You two seemed to be having a grand ole time."

"Excuse me?"

"I noticed you two were having a lot of fun catching up."

"Greg and I used to be pretty good friends. I haven't seen him in a few years. He's hilarious."

Hilarious. "I remember he was pretty funny back in high school as well. Did he tell you he got divorced?"

"He did."

"Funny and single."

She scrunched up her face. "Okay…"

"I'm going to go shop again and let you wrap without distraction like I'm supposed to." He walked away but had to come back to get a new list. He could feel his cheeks warm from embarrassment.

"Dr. Drake, fancy meeting you here." Janet Williams had her arms full.

"Can I help you with that?" he said, taking a couple of the gifts off the top.

"Thank you. You are such a gentleman."

"Are you ready to go to the wrapping table or do you need to keep shopping?"

"I need something for—" she referenced her list "—a six-year-old boy."

"I know where those toys are. Follow me." He led her over to the five-and-six-year-old boys section.

"It says he likes trucks. Are there any trucks left?"

Jonah dug around a bit and found a fire truck that lit up and made noise. "He's going to love this. What else?"

"He also likes art and something called a squishy." Janet made a face before cracking up.

Jonah laughed. He had no idea what a squishy was. "They have all the art supplies over there," he said, pointing in the direction of the table they set up with all the coloring books, markers, crayons and paint.

Janet went and grabbed some markers and a coloring book about trucks. Jonah asked one of the women shopping by the twelve-year-old girls if she knew what a squishy was.

"It's a kind of stuffed animal," he reported to Janet, handing her one that looked like a tiger.

"You are amazing. Always a problem-solver. I need to keep you around more often."

He helped her get everything to the wrapping table. Greg was nowhere to be seen, thankfully. Holly was still finishing the gifts he had brought over there a few minutes before. She was scowling at the package in front of her. She tried to tear off a piece of tape from the dispenser and got frustrated when it wouldn't come off.

Jonah and Janet set their pile of gifts in front of his grandmother. "Do your best with these, Gran."

"You know I will."

Janet thanked him for helping her again. "I feel like I should return the favor. Can I help you shop your list?"

"This one is easy, but I will find you if I need some help later on."

Her smile fell. "Oh, okay."

Jonah left to do his shopping. He ended up in the same section as Greg. He was digging around for an action figure. "I wish I would have picked wrapping. I wouldn't have to do as much thinking. Do you think they'd let us switch jobs?"

It was clear why Greg wanted to switch

jobs. "No, I don't think they want people switching. Plus there's nowhere to sit over there."

"Can you believe Holly Hayward is here? I didn't know she went to this church. Guess I need to pay better attention during services to see who's there."

"She doesn't go to church here. She's here because she came with her great-uncle who is marrying my grandmother."

"Oh, wow. You and Holly are going to be related?"

"We won't be related."

"Her uncle is going to be your step-grandpa. That makes you, like, her second cousin or something."

"She's not going to be my cousin, Greg."

"Right. I mean it's just by marriage. You could still totally make out with her if you wanted to, but you guys hated each other in school, didn't you?"

"I didn't hate anyone," Jonah said clearly. The only thing he'd ever felt about Holly was confused. Not too different from how he felt now.

"That's right. I think it was Holly who

hated you. Her family had a thing against your family or something."

Jonah felt like he was going to explode. He needed to get out of the section. He needed to get out of this church. He needed some fresh air. Without a jacket, he escaped outside and took a couple of deep breaths. The cold air felt good in his lungs and helped cool his temper. Holly hated him. She hated his family. They had always been and would forever be at odds with one another.

"Jonah!" He turned around and there was Holly holding his jacket in her hands.

CHAPTER FOURTEEN

"ARE YOU OKAY?"

Jonah's chest rose and fell with heavy breaths like he had just run a marathon. It was so cold out, she could see his breath like a cloud around his face.

"I'm fine. You can go back inside. Please go back inside."

She didn't turn away. She handed him his coat. "It's freezing out here. Are you leaving?"

"I needed a minute alone, but apparently I can't get that even out here." His tone was sharp like he was angry with her. He slipped his arms into his coat.

"Sorry, I suppose you were hoping Janet would be the one to bring you your coat," she snapped back.

"Why would I want Janet to come out here if I wanted to be alone?"

"I don't know, you seemed to be having

a great time gathering gifts with her. She was all hahahaha." She ran her hand down his arm, mimicking Janet. "'Oh, Dr. Drake, you must work out. You're so handsome and strong.'"

"Oh, wow. I'm surprised you even noticed Janet or anyone else was even here. You were so enthralled with Greg and his hilariousness."

Why was he so fixated on Greg? She had talked to him for a couple of minutes. "Sorry I have a sense of humor and laugh at funny things people say. I didn't know that would bother you so much."

"It doesn't bother me. You can laugh all you want with whomever you want. I sure as heck know you don't want to do that with me. You've made that clear. In fact, you've made that clear since the moment we met. Even Greg was aware of the fact that you hate me."

Holly rubbed her forehead. "What are you talking about? I have never talked about you with Greg. And I don't hate you. You know I don't hate you."

"But you can't give me a chance because you hate my great-grandfather or maybe it's my great-great-grandfather. I'm not sure which one ruined your life. The one who promised the land and died without putting that in writing or the one who sold the land to someone else because it wasn't in writing that it was supposed to be given to your family."

Holly let out a long sigh. "Well, forgive me for not being able to shut off my feelings like they're on a light switch. I also can't help it that you come from a family that did us wrong. I know it's not your fault, but—"

"But what? It's not my fault, but I have to pay for it. I don't know what to do with that."

Holly closed her eyes and tilted her face to the sky. She knew it was irrational, but her feelings were real. Her dad's feelings were real. And they weren't something that could be changed in an instant. She needed time, and she wasn't sure there was enough time for her dad to come around.

She opened her eyes and faced him. "I don't want to fight with you. I don't want to argue with you in a parking lot about things that can't be solved by yelling about them."

"I don't want to fight with you, either. I want to take you out to dinner. I want to know what your favorite movie is and how you got that little scar above your right eyebrow. I want to feel the way you make me feel when you smile at me. I want to bet you that I can treat you better than Greg or any other guy in the world because I care about things like that."

Her breaths quickened. No one had ever said things like that to her before. She wanted to cry because of the intensity of these feelings. Jonah wasn't whom she thought she should be with. He was the kind of man she dreamed about, but did she deserve him?

"I—" she started, but her phone rang. She pulled it out of her pocket to silence it until she noticed it was her dad. She stepped away a couple of feet and answered it. "Dad?"

"I talked to Frank. We figured it out. I need you to get back to the bar ASAP. Can you get Randall to drive you back or do you want me to send Frank to pick you up?"

"I can ask Randall."

"Wait, no, don't," he said, quickly changing his mind. "I need him to stay where he is so we can talk to you in private. I'll send Frank. This is a great plan, honey."

There was no telling what those two had

brainstormed. She was afraid to find out, but curious simultaneously. She ended the call and found Jonah raking his fingers through his hair.

"Forget what I said. I think I need to go home. It's been a long day and I'm tired. I'm also tired of all this wedding sabotage. I don't care if my grandmother marries Randall. I don't care if that makes us cousins or whatever it makes us. I just want to go home. Can you tell my gran that I went home?"

"Jonah," she said, trying to stop him, but he found his keys in his pocket and headed right for his truck.

It was better that she let him go. All she did was hurt him and that wasn't fair. She went inside to tell Randall she was leaving and let Clarissa know Jonah had left.

She ran into Janet before she could get to anyone else. "Is Jonah okay?"

"He's going home. He said he's really tired."

"Oh." She tugged at her earlobe. "You're really blowing this, you know?"

Janet had been right from the beginning. Jonah was a perfect catch. Just like she was completely correct now.

"I know," Holly whispered. She went to find Randall and Clarissa, who were confused but wished her a good evening anyway.

Greg stopped her on her way out. "Where are you going in such a hurry?"

"I've got to get back to the Roadrunner."

"You're going to the Roadrunner? Maybe I should sneak out of here and join you. I could use a drink or two."

"I'm going back to work, Greg. But you're welcome anytime. In fact, we're having a New Year's Eve party. You should find a date and buy some tickets. My ride's here. I'll see you later." She slipped past him and out the door.

Frank drove her back to the bar. As soon as she arrived, her dad ushered her into the office in the back.

"We figured it out," Frank said.

"It's the perfect plan," Will said. "He basically handed it to us on a silver platter today and I didn't even notice it until I was telling Frank what he said."

"What are you talking about?" She was tired of deciphering others today.

Will stroked his beard. "He told us that he

doesn't have time for people who attack his family. If someone came after someone in his family, he would go to bat for that person. We need him to go to bat for us."

"And how do you propose we get him to go to bat for one of us against Clarissa?"

"We got it all planned out," Frank said, rubbing his hands together as if he was the villain in this particular story.

"That's where you come into play. You see, Randall loves you. He thinks you are totally on board with this wedding, so he would never think you'd do it."

"Do what?"

Frank sat on the edge of his seat. "You're going to steal something from the Drake ranch, but you're going to deny it. When you deny it, Randall's going to jump to your defense."

"And then he's going to hate me when he finds out that I really did steal it."

"No, he won't find out you stole it because it's going to reappear because we're going to put it back," Will explained.

Frank continued, "So when they accuse you and talk bad about you, Randall won't stand for it and he'll call the wedding off."

This was a terrible plan. "You want me to steal from the Drake ranch. What am I stealing exactly? How are they going to know it was me? How do we get Clarissa to be the one who accuses me? What if Randall believes them instead of me? They will be the ones telling the truth."

"Stop poking holes in our perfect plan," Frank whined. "It will work if you just try."

"Remember when we were talking about stealing invites out of mailboxes?" her dad asked. "What if we do like you said and have you offer to mail the invites but don't mail them. When people start to say their invites didn't show up, they're going to blame you because you offered to mail them."

"You want me to steal the invites?"

"It was your idea in the first place, so you can't deny that it's a great plan," Will said.

Holly had been so close to being done with all this. She had resolved to letting Randall and Clarissa have their big day in peace.

"She told me today she just finished addressing all the invites and plans to take them to the post office tomorrow."

"See? It's meant to be." Her dad was so

proud of himself. "You'll go over there tomorrow and offer to take them to the post office for her. You'll need to get there early. We don't want her to drop them off before you get there."

"Fine, but if this doesn't work, you need to let this happen and you need to be kind to Clarissa. Do you think you can do that?"

Frank and Will exchanged glances. "We won't have to. This is going to work."

"I'm not doing it until you make that deal."

"Fine," her dad grumbled. "If it doesn't work, I'll welcome her into the family."

It didn't feel completely sincere, but it was going to have to do.

JONAH HAD NO PLAN. He left the church with no idea what he was going to do other than go home and pout. He was a grown man and he was pouting.

His uncle's car was parked outside the house when he got home, though. He was sitting inside all by himself.

"Oliver?" Jonah called out when he stepped inside.

"There you are. I've been looking all over for you."

"I was with Gran and Mom at the church helping with the toy drive. What's going on?"

"I've figured out how we can stop this wedding. I'm going to need your help."

Jonah was over this. He wasn't going to ruin his grandmother's happiness. "I don't want to stop the wedding anymore."

"Oh, really? Do you seriously want her to marry Randall Hayward?"

"Randall has been nothing but good to her. They get along and I have never seen her this happy."

Oliver took a seat and drummed his fingers on the arm of the chair. "You think all of the Haywards are ready to welcome your grandmother into their family? Do you think they are going to treat her with the kind of respect she deserves?"

Most of the Haywards had been nothing but nice to Gran, but it was Holly herself who said her father and others in the family were never going to be okay with this marriage. She didn't think her dad could ever get over what happened to his grandfather.

"You're hesitating," Oliver said, sitting

forward in his seat. "What makes you hesitate?"

"I don't know. There are some Haywards who can't let it go that your grandfather refused to give them some land."

"Oh, man! That again? Those people are ridiculous. They act like because their granddad worked on our ranch, we should have just handed over some land to them for free? Should I go tell Carter he can have a few acres?"

"Well, it was a little more complicated than that," Jonah said.

"These people can't stand it that we have worked hard and been successful. I don't know why their failure to make money is somehow our fault. If they are going to treat my mother as if she's some kind of enemy, I have to stop this. You have to stop this."

Maybe they wouldn't be mean to her face, but it was possible that their resentments would start to seep out into their interactions with her. She would pick up on it and it would eat at her. He didn't want his grandmother to feel that way.

"What kind of plan have you come up with?"

"Randall Hayward has had more girl-friends than I've sold cars. This man doesn't know how to be in a committed relationship. I would prefer my mother figure that out now rather than after she marries the guy."

"And how do you plan to do that?"

"We're going to tempt Randall until he breaks. Haven't you ever watched those talk shows where they send in an under-cover woman to hit on a married guy to see if he'll cheat or not?"

"You're going to hire someone to hit on him?"

"It's a fast-and-easy way to get him to re-veal his true nature."

"What if he doesn't take the bait?"

"He'll take the bait."

Jonah wasn't so sure. Randall seemed so in love. Someone in love didn't cheat. Maybe Oliver would change his opinion of Randall if he passed this test.

"What do you need me to do?"

"I need you to help me get him alone. We can't have your grandmother anywhere around when we do this. I was thinking we could do it at the Hot Chocolate Fest. There will be a lot of people around. He won't suspect an unfamiliar face."

Hot Chocolate Fest was this weekend. One week before the wedding. Nothing like waiting until the last minute.

"Fine, but if this doesn't work, you need to give me your word that you're going to let Gran be happy and if being with Randall is what she thinks is going to make her happy, marrying Randall is what she's going to do."

"I'm not worried. This will work."

"But if it doesn't…"

Oliver sighed dramatically. "If it doesn't, I'll happily walk my mother down the aisle. How's that?"

Oliver had a deal. Jonah wondered what Holly would think of all this. She probably still wanted this wedding to be stopped, so she'd probably think it was a good idea. Of course, if it worked, it would be because they outed Randall as a cheat. Something told him she wouldn't like that. The Drakes were the bad guys in her story. If it turned out her family was in the wrong, she'd probably flip out.

They were going to find out in a few days. Jonah saw his uncle out and went to bed.

The sooner they got to Christmas, the better. He didn't care how it ended; he just wanted it all to be over.

The next morning, his grandmother and his mother were talking about baking a wedding cake when Jonah came down to make coffee.

"It can't be that hard," Gran said. "It doesn't need to be that big. We aren't having that many people."

"If it's small, I would think a bakery could make it with a little more than a week's notice," his mother said.

"You didn't order a cake?" Jonah was surprised she hadn't taken care of that earlier.

"I was thinking that a cake would be a nice way for me to do something special for Randall. I thought I'd ask Holly what his favorite flavor was and surprise him by making it myself."

"That's very sweet, Gran. I'm sure he'll love whatever you do."

The doorbell rang and all three of them froze. No one was expecting anyone this early. Jonah offered to go answer it. He absolutely was not expecting Holly, but his heart did that dumb little jump it did whenever he saw her.

For a moment, he thought maybe she came to tell him she had thought about what he said to her and she was here to beg him for a second chance.

"Hey, is your grandmother here?"

He felt the disappointment deeper than he expected. "It's eight in the morning. She's here."

"Right. Sorry. May I talk to her?"

"Sure. Is everything okay?"

Holly fidgeted with the sleeve of her coat. "Yeah, everything is fine. Are you fine?"

That was a loaded question he was not answering. "Why don't you come in. I just put on some coffee."

Holly stepped inside and let him take her coat. He led her back to the kitchen. "Holly's here for you, Gran."

Gran had her join them at the kitchen table. "Your ears must have been burning. We were just talking about you."

Her eyes flashed to Jonah. "She was talking about you. Why don't you tell her what you were talking about?" he asked his grand-

mother so she didn't think that he was shar-
ing anything about her with them.

"I was just saying I should ask you if you
know what Randall's favorite cake flavor
is. I think I'd like to surprise him by making our wedding cake. Do you think that's
a good idea?"

Holly pressed her hand to her chest. "I
think that's a very nice idea. Randall will
love it. He's a big red velvet fan. We always
get that for him on his birthday."

"Perfect. Thank you so much. I knew I
could count on you."

Holly avoided eye contact and tucked some
of her hair behind her ear. Jonah wondered
why that made her so uncomfortable. He
handed her a cup of coffee.

"Now, what can I do for you?" Gran asked.

"Um, I was planning on finalizing some
of the plans for the reception and I just
wanted to double-check a couple things
about the menu."

Jonah found it strange that she came all
this way to ask a question about the reception. She could have called. He didn't want
to hope, but maybe she wanted to see him.

He listened to them chat about the menu

for a few minutes and then Holly was on her feet. "Well, I don't want to take up any more of your morning. I need to stop by the post office on my way to the Roadrunner, so I better head out."

"You're going to the post office?"

"I am. Did you need me to drop something off for you?"

"The invitations to the wedding!" Gran exclaimed. She got up and disappeared into the other room, returning with a stack of envelopes. "If you could drop these off, I would be forever grateful. Save me the trip."

"Of course," Holly said, taking the invitations. "Happy to help."

Something didn't sit right. "The post office is out of your way if you're heading to work. The post office is actually on the way to the clinic. Why don't you give me what you have to drop off and the invitations and I'll stop at the post office on my way to work?" Jonah offered.

"No, I got it. It's not that much out of the way. Plus, I have lots of time before I need to be at work. Plenty of time to go to the post office."

"Really, it's not a big deal. I drive right by it."

Holly backed away, moving toward the foyer. "I need to take my packages in and pay for the postage, so I need to go."

"You can pay me back. I don't mind." Jonah remembered something Holly had said when they were at the rodeo and they were both still actively trying to stop this wedding from happening. She had a plan to offer to mail the invites and not mail them.

"I've got it, Jonah. Really, it's fine."

"Well, thank you again for doing that. And thank you for the red velvet suggestion," Gran said.

"Have a good day, everybody," Holly said.

"I'll see you out," Jonah said, stepping aside so she could go first.

"I know the way."

"I'll see you out," he repeated. As soon as they made it to the front door, he dropped the pretenses. "Are you mailing those invites?"

"What do you mean?"

"You know what I mean. Are you mailing them or is this part of your plan to stop this wedding from happening?"

"I'm mailing them," she said completely unconvincingly.

"You showed up here at eight in the morning to ask a question that could have been answered over the phone and then just happened to be going to the post office. Is red velvet even Randall's favorite cake flavor? Is he allergic and you're going to make my grandmother put him into anaphylactic shock?"

"What? No! Why would I do that? Randall loves red velvet. You can ask him yourself if you don't believe me."

"I might just do that."

"Go ahead."

"Maybe I'll follow you to the post office, make sure you mail those invites."

"Maybe I'm not going straight to the post office. Maybe I have other errands to run."

Jonah folded his arms in front of his chest. "I'm on to you."

"And if you were innocent, I would be worried."

She said it as if she knew what he was going to do this weekend at Hot Chocolate Fest. Neither one of them was innocent. If he called her out in front of his grandmother, she could easily tell Gran about the things he had done. She would never forgive him, and she shouldn't.

He watched Holly walk to her car. He once again couldn't wait for this to be over. One way or another, come Christmas Day, he was going to be done.

CHAPTER FIFTEEN

HOLLY COULDN'T REMEMBER a time she felt worse about herself. Even when she was a moody teenager, she liked herself more than she did right now. Clarissa was an absolute sweetheart of a person. Jonah was lucky to have such a wonderful grandmother.

"What else do we need?" Maisy reviewed the hot chocolate bar ingredients one more time. They had gotten a booth at the Hot Chocolate Festival today. They were going to be selling three kinds of hot chocolate— a traditional hot cocoa, a grown-up version with a shot of Bailey's and a chocolate peppermint with peppermint whipped cream. The last one was Holly's favorite.

"I think we have everything we need. It's going to be great."

"Danny is bringing the kids by at six. Based on how things are going, I might just leave with them. Do you have a problem with that?"

"You're a pregnant mother of two. You should leave whenever you want to." Holly was amazed by her sister. She was a super-woman.

"I promise I won't leave you high and dry. If it's really busy, I'll stay."

"We'll figure it out, I'm not worried."

"Do you have all the cups?" their dad asked as soon as Holly closed the trunk of her sister's minivan.

"We have everything," Holly assured him.

Hot Chocolate Fest in Coyote at Christ-mastime was like a local craft beer fest in the summertime. At least twenty local res-taurants and businesses participated. The whole town came out to taste-test all the different variations of hot chocolate. Some were gourmet and she was sure some oth-ers were just powdered mix packets from the grocery store.

"What's going on with you?" Maisy asked as soon as they hit the road. "You've been weirdly quiet the last couple days. Should I be worried?"

If Holly confessed all the things that were

making her not herself, her sister would probably disown her. "Nothing to worry about. Everything is fine."

"Are things okay with you and Jonah?"

"There are no things with me and Jonah so I don't know what you're talking about."

"So that's what's wrong. I thought things were going well. You two were really cute together."

Maisy had no clue how much torture this conversation was going to be. "We were not together. We will never be together. Jonah and I are not even friends."

"If you're saying that because his last name is Drake, I will seriously put you in time-out like I do when Gia and Patrick are being boneheads."

"Have you and Danny talked about possible names for the new baby?" Holly asked, desperate to change the subject. "I was thinking if it's a girl, you could name her after me since I'm sure to be her favorite aunt."

"Tell me one thing that makes you and Jonah incompatible. If you can tell me one thing, I'll leave you alone. And it can't be that he's a Drake and you're a Hayward.

Uncle Randall has already proven that does not matter."

"He's super smart and I'm not."

"You are plenty smart. You could have gone to college if you had wanted to, but you chose to work for dad and learn the business side. One day, you're going to be running the Roadrunner and a not-smart person could not do that. Try again."

Holly stared out the window, counting the blocks they had left before they would arrive and have to set up.

"You can't think of anything. Just admit it."

"There are so many things, I don't know where to start. He likes to do things like ice-skate and ski. Things I've done like once in my life. I'm sure he would rather spend his time with people who enjoy the same activities that he does."

"You would probably love skiing if you did it more often. You're the perfect daredevil for that kind of sport. Plus, Danny likes to compete in fantasy football and I don't. Just because he has an interest in something I don't doesn't make us incompatible."

Holly gave up. There was nothing she was

going to say that would convince Maisy that they didn't belong together. "I don't know, Maisy. All I can tell you is that we are not going to ever date one another. We don't like each other in that way."

"Are you intentionally lying to me or unaware that you're lying to yourself?"

She was unbelievable. Thankfully, they had arrived at their destination and it was time to get ready for the fest. The town square was going to be shut down to traffic, so the booths were going to be set up on the parkways between the street and the sidewalk as well as around the Christmas tree in the square.

The Roadrunner had been assigned one of the corner spots, which seemed like a good thing. They started setting up their tent. Holly had talked her dad into investing in a custom, professionally branded tailgating tent. They had a Roadrunner-branded tablecloth to cover the table that would separate them from the customers. There were also two banners and some cool swag to pass out. It was all about getting the Roadrunner's name out there so more people frequented the bar and grill.

"Wow, this is quite a step up from last year," Wayne Larson said. He was the owner of the local coffee shop, Cool Beans.

"I convinced my dad we needed it. We got these stickers and pens, too. We're fancy this year," Holly said, handing him a pen with the Roadrunner's name, address and phone number on it.

"Good idea. Any chance you'd be willing to share the name of the company you used?"

"For you, Wayne, anything. Give me your email and I'll send you their contact information."

Wayne rattled off his email so Holly could share her resources. Wayne wasn't the only one to compliment their setup. Several of the other people around them came over to check it out.

"I told you you're smart," Maisy said.

Holly didn't want to think about Jonah. She wanted to focus on the event and being a positive face for the business. If she could sell out of hot chocolate, she could leave early with Maisy. They were set up on time and ready when the people started rolling in. The sisters were so busy in the first hour,

Holly didn't notice that Jonah was in their line until he was behind the person she was waiting on.

"Did you mail the invites?" he asked her when he got up to the front.

"Did you want some hot chocolate? We have three flavors. All of them taste delicious and will warm you up," she deflected.

"Holly…"

"Jonah, this is a hot chocolate booth. If you want my attention, you need to buy a hot chocolate."

"Fine, I'll take a regular hot chocolate and I want to know what day you mailed the invites because my grandmother is losing her mind over it."

"What invites?" Maisy asked.

"The wedding invites. Holly came over the other day and took the invitations from my grandma, saying she was already going to the post office and could take care of it for her. At the time, it seemed awfully generous."

He was rightfully suspicious. It made Holly sick to her stomach to know that the invites were sitting in a drawer in Will's office, waiting for this confrontation to take place. Only, it was supposed to be Clarissa and Randall.

"You mailed out the wedding invitations? I didn't get one," Maisy said. She squirted some whipped cream on top of her customer's hot chocolate before handing it to him. "When did you take them to the post office?"

"Did you go to the post office on Wednesday when you said you were going?" Jonah asked.

"Wednesday? It usually only takes a day for things to get where they're supposed to be when it's local. You don't think the post office lost them, do you?" Maisy asked innocently.

"Can we talk when things aren't so busy? I need to keep this line moving."

Jonah didn't need to talk to her later. Her refusal to answer was answer enough. She had shared this plan with him once before. "I get what's happening here. I don't need to bother you later."

It would have been nice to explain, so he wasn't so angry with her. She couldn't do that with Maisy standing next to her because then she'd have to explain all the other things they'd been doing.

Jonah left and the rest of the night flew by. Randall, Howie, Frank and Old Red showed up and bought one of each flavor they were selling. Holly was surprised that Clarissa wasn't with Randall, but he said Jonah had encouraged them to make this a boys'-night-out event. It seemed clear that Jonah was no longer interested in trying to stop the wedding or putting his grandmother in situations that made her uncomfortable. She didn't blame him. It hadn't worked and she hoped that this last-ditch effort by her dad would also fail.

By the time Danny and the kids showed up, they were almost sold out. Maisy offered to help her finish up and break things down.

"Have you been worrying about the invites this whole time?" Maisy asked as they started packing up. "If the post office messed up, that's not on you. Uncle Randall will understand. We can figure out how to get a hold of everyone. We probably should have showed them how to email invites with it being so close to the wedding."

Holly's only option was to avoid Maisy's

questions and try to find Jonah. "If you want to just take everything home, I can help you unload it at work tomorrow. I'm going to hang out here a little bit longer."

"Yeah." Maisy nudged her with her elbow. "Maybe Jonah can give you a ride home."

Unlikely. "I'll ask him," Holly replied, forcing a smile. "See you tomorrow."

"Have a good night. Stay positive and get out of your own way." Her sister was full of relationship advice. Holly nodded and gave her a thumbs-up.

The string lights crisscrossing the street and on the trees in the square usually made it feel like Holly was in the night sky with all the stars, but tonight, it felt like she was in a giant interrogation room and the lights were there to expose her lies. She walked around, looking for Jonah. They had an area set up with some outdoor patio heaters and some pub tables for people to stand around. That was where she found Jonah with Randall.

JONAH CHECKED HIS watch for the third time in a span of a few minutes. Oliver had arranged for the woman to show up at seven thirty and it was a quarter to eight. Maybe she had backed out and Jonah could go home and forget all about this plan.

Randall was a social creature. All night long, he'd had people coming up to talk to him. Men and women alike were interested in either his big lottery win or his impending marriage. He was nice to everyone and no nicer to the women than he was to the men. Jonah did not believe this plan was going to work. His hope was that when this failed, it would finally get Oliver off his back.

"Doesn't this group look like trouble?" The sound of Holly's voice caused Jonah to spin around. It was so strange to be so angry with someone and so happy to see her at the same time.

"Trouble? We're at the most PG drinking fest in all of Colorado. I don't think we could find trouble if we tried," Old Red joked.

"You sold out fast," Randall said, welcoming his grandniece with a side hug. "Next year, we'll have to get you some bigger hot water storage jugs so you can sell more."

Jonah did not want Holly here when the trap showed up. She'd smell a fraud a mile away. Randall was also less likely to take the bait with her or him around for that matter.

"Can I talk to you for a second? In private?"

"In private?" Howie put his arm around Holly. "I don't know. Can we trust our niece around this guy?"

"Let them be. He's good for her and she's good for him," Randall said. "His grandmother and I are waiting to take credit for this little match made in heaven."

Jonah hated to burst his bubble. Even though she thought she was the most like him, she couldn't get past the past like he had. He motioned for Holly to follow him away from the group. She followed without hesitation. He knew she had some explaining to do.

"Can I start?" she asked. When he nodded, she dived right in. "I know you're mad at me for a bunch of reasons, and I don't blame you."

"I just need to know if my myriad of reasons should include stealing the wedding invitations."

"Well, Mr. Fancy Talker, I have no clue what a myriad means, but I am guessing my answer is yes, but I'm planning on sending them. They just need to go out a little late so we can see what reaction we get."

"Who is *we*?"

"This is my dad's final test. If your grandma can be cool about this, then my dad and Frank have agreed to back off."

"Frank is in on this, too?" Jonah wouldn't have guessed he was against it given the way he always agreed with Randall when they were together.

"I know you're done with trying to mess things up, and honestly, so am I. Please believe me, I feel bad. I don't like that it means stressing Clarissa out before her wedding."

"It's majorly stressing her out. She keeps asking her friends if they got it and no one has, obviously. She's only inviting a handful of her friends and family. She's not worried about them, she's spoken to all of them and they know it's on Christmas Day at the ranch. She's in a panic that Randall's friends won't get the invite and will think she didn't invite them, leading to some hard feelings."

She rubbed her forehead. "Ugh. I don't want to do this anymore. I just want Christmas to come and go."

"I feel the same way. I want this to be over."

Jonah noticed two women stopping to talk to Randall and his friends. One of them was wearing the bright pink jacket Jonah was told to be on the lookout for. This was it. The trap was set. He prayed that Randall didn't fall for it.

"I wish I was done messing with things like you are. That has to be such a relief."

He should have come clean but something stopped him from telling her what he was up to. It probably had something to do with the fact that he was a giant hypocrite. It wouldn't matter his excuse, she would not forgive him for being hard on her when he was doing something just as duplicitous.

"How did things go from fun and games to making us both feel miserable?"

She toyed with a lock of her hair. "I don't know. I miss when the worst thing to happen was losing a bet to you."

He leaned against the nearest pub table, resting his chin on the palm of his hand. "I miss beating you. Those were the good old days."

"Don't act like there were a lot of those days. We were neck and neck."

"Oh, don't worry, I am well aware that you were keeping score and know exactly how many times you won and I lost," he said with a laugh.

"I'm good at keeping score. Maybe too good. I need a shorter memory."

"I wish I knew how to get you one." He wanted to wrap his arms around her and hold her against him until she forgot all about these old rivalries and family dramas. If they could just focus on him and her, what a wonderful world it would be.

Holly's gaze drifted back toward Randall and his crew. "Who are those women talking to Randall? Do you recognize them?"

"I don't know," he lied. "Probably somebody who heard he won the lottery. That seemed to be a hot topic earlier."

"I hate people who only care about the money. I feel like I should go over there and rescue him."

"Randall handles people like that without too much trouble. I wouldn't worry about him."

Holly was undeterred; she began to make

her way back to the group. Jonah chased after her, gently wrapping his hand around her arm to stop her. "Stay with me," he begged.

Her cheeks turned red and he heard her breathing hitch. "I don't want to hurt you anymore," she said. "I don't know why someone like you cares at all about someone like me."

"What are you talking about?"

"I don't deserve someone like you. You are just like your grandmother. You're kind and patient. You always do things for the right reasons. You tolerate all my faults, then turn around and put up with me when I attack you for the smallest things."

"I haven't felt attacked by you."

"See? You selectively forget when I've been mean."

"You're not mean."

"The day Randall and Clarissa got engaged, you were afraid I was going to be mean to your grandmother. That had to be based off how I treated you growing up. I can be mean. I hold grudges. You deserve better."

"What I deserve is to be happy and to

laugh. I deserve to have fun and remember what it's like to be young instead of being so serious all the time. You bring all those good things into my life. You make me smile. Everyone says so. It's like I must have been the grumpiest person in the world before we started hanging out."

She drew her bottom lip between her teeth and shook her head. Her eyes were wet with unshed tears. "I don't know why you think that. I have been nothing but a pain. I should go."

She slipped out of his grasp and disappeared into the crowd. She might not know why he thought what he said was true, but he did. He noticed the woman in the pink jacket invading Randall's personal space. Jonah wasn't the angel she painted him to be. He had done things he wasn't proud of and wasn't honest about it. They were both flawed. The only way to prove to her that was true was by being honest.

That was what he was going to do.

CHAPTER SIXTEEN

"I'VE GOT RANDALL coming in hot in five minutes. He's on his way over here right now. We're putting Operation Defend Your Family into action right now. Everyone get ready." Will was determined to make his plan work. Even though Clarissa hadn't accused Holly of any wrongdoing, her dad was ready to stir the pot, make some accusations of his own and put some words in Clarissa's mouth.

Holly hated everything about this plan. Ever since she left the Hot Chocolate Fest last night, she wanted to out this plan to Randall. She didn't see how being deceitful was the right thing to do. They were literally being the bad guys. Manipulating the system. Lying, cheating. This was no longer for the greater good; this was simply about winning.

"He asked me again if I got an invite to

the wedding and I said no. She must be putting the heat on him, and she has to be thinking that Holly didn't follow through."

"I told him last night that it seemed strange that we didn't get the invite and he said Clarissa had theories. Not one theory. Theories, plural. One of them has to be putting the blame on Holly," Frank said.

"And she would be right," Holly said, frustrated with their nonsense. "I am to blame. I don't know why we're trying to ruin this woman's relationship with a really great guy like Uncle Randall because she is right about me being a bad person."

Panic flashed across her dad's face. "Okay, you cannot say any of that when he comes in."

"Why are we doing this? Why don't you want Uncle Randall to be happy with someone he cares about?"

"Drakes and Haywards cannot peacefully coexist, Holly. You know this."

"I don't know it, Dad. In fact, I've spent the last three weeks learning that the exact opposite is true. Randall and Clarissa get along beautifully. Mom, Yvonne and Maisy got along great with Clarissa, her granddaughter and with Jonah's mom when we were there for breakfast. We all got along when we came back here after the Frontier Freeze. You both were here and I watched you and people with the last name Drake get along just fine."

"I don't know where this attitude is coming from, but you need to pull it together. We are this close to saving your uncle from making the biggest mistake of his life."

"Maybe I think the biggest mistake would be him not getting married to Clarissa. Maybe being tricked into defending someone who doesn't deserve it is the biggest mistake he could make."

"She can't be here when he gets here," Frank said. "She's going to ruin everything. Maybe it's better if she's not here. We can say she's so upset about being judged, she couldn't even talk to him about it."

Holly slammed her hand on the counter. "I'm standing right here."

Before they could get rid of her, Randall came waltzing in. "Just the person I was looking for. Do you remember who was working behind the counter at the post office when you dropped off the invitations? Was it a man or a woman? Tall or short? Whatever description you can give me would help."

"Why are you interrogating my daughter like she's some sort of criminal? Are you insinuating that she had something to do with it?" Her dad's fake outrage was too much.

"I'm not insinuating anything except that I think someone in the post office messed up."

"It sounds like someone else might think that it was Holly who messed up. Has Clarissa been pointing fingers at my daughter?"

"Of course not. She knows Holly is a sweetheart."

"That's not what we heard," Frank said, throwing his hands up.

Randall scratched his head. "What did you hear exactly?"

"They heard nothing," Holly said, having enough. She went back into her dad's office. She could hear Frank trying to sell the story that she was so distraught by the lies being told about her by Drakes that she had to go in the back and cry. She returned with the stack of invites.

"I didn't mail them. I should have mailed them, but I was trying to make these two happy by sabotaging your wedding."

"You were trying to sabotage my wedding?"

"I tried to make the two of you realize you were incompatible, but that failed miserably. So, I moved on to sabotaging the wedding plans."

"You didn't order any of that stuff for the reception, did you?"

"No, I did. I swear. Everything is ready to go for the reception."

Randall raked his fingers through his hair. "How am I supposed to trust that?"

She didn't blame him for his lack of faith in her. She had earned his distrust. "I have all the receipts. I'm standing here, coming clean. I don't want to ruin your wedding."

"You don't want to ruin my wedding?" He gave a bitter laugh. "Today? But yesterday and all the days before, it seems like you kinda wanted to ruin my wedding."

"I know. And I am sorry. I can't tell you how sorry I am. I've been carrying around this mountain of regret. I like Clarissa. She is lovely. She is perfect for you."

Randall's hands tightened into fists. "But this is how you treat her?" He knocked the pile of invitations across the bar just as Maisy walked in.

"What is going on?" Maisy bent down and picked up one of the envelopes. "Are these the invitations? Did they finally make it?"

"They didn't make it anywhere but your father's office," Randall said. He pointed at Frank and Will. "You two disappoint me more than I can say. To think that you've been plotting behind my back while you smile in my face. How am I ever going to trust you? Why would I want to?"

"We were trying to protect you," Will asserted. "No one with the last name Drake can be trusted. For all we know, Oliver could be plotting a way to steal your money."

"You're going to stand here and accuse Oliver of being deceitful when the only people who have been lying are in this room and are my flesh and blood?"

"Holly, what is going on?" Maisy asked, picking up the invitations that Randall scattered across the room. "I thought you mailed these for them."

"I lied."

"Why? What was the purpose?"

"They were trying to ruin my wedding."

"We were trying to bait someone from Clarissa's family into accusing me of not mailing them so Uncle Randall would come to my defense and break it off with Clarissa."

"That was the plan? You two must have come up with that." Maisy pointed at Frank and her dad. "That is the worst plan I have ever heard in my life. Why would Randall defend her when she was guilty?"

"It was a bad plan," Holly acknowledged.

"Wait until Mom hears about this."

"You leave your mother out of this, Maisy Marie," Will demanded.

"Maisy and Bonnie had no idea?" Randall asked Holly.

She shook her head.

"What about Yvonne and Howie?"

Frank shook his head.

"It was just us," Holly said.

"Jonah knew," Will tattled.

Holly shot him an icy glare. There was no reason to throw Jonah under the bus.

"Jonah was a part of this?"

"He was part of it in the beginning when all we were doing was making sure you and Clarissa spent time together. We thought that the more time you spent together, the more you'd recognize you had too many differences. Jonah hasn't been involved in anything since the Frontier Freeze."

"You thought that if you forced Clarissa to come to the Frontier Freeze, she'd break up with me?"

"By that time, it was clear that you were both too in love. We had higher hopes when you went to the gingerbread contest and she came to the rodeo."

"All of those events. All that fun we had. You were hoping we'd break up while it was happening."

Holly hung her head, unable to look him in the eye she was so ashamed.

"I'm so sorry, Uncle Randall," Maisy said. "I feel like an idiot. They were all so against the idea and then did a quick one-eighty. I should have known."

"It's not your fault, honey. You tell your mother I am not mad at her one bit. Holly, come with me. Let's go," he said with a snap of his fingers.

Holly didn't bother to look to her dad for permission to leave before her shift. She grabbed her coat and followed him out.

"Where are we going?" she asked, fearing the worst and trying to keep up with his hurried pace.

"You're going to fess up to Clarissa."

JONAH HAD SPENT the entire morning in bed. It wasn't like him to be such a bum. He had never taken a sick day before, but today was the first. Lovesick. That was what he was and it seemed as good as any reason to stay home in bed.

His mom knocked on his door. "Can I get you anything? Do you want some water or I could make you some toast. Is it your stomach?"

He shook his head. It was his heart. It was broken and he didn't have a remedy to fix it.

"If you change your mind, I guess you can text me. Next year, you better take it easy on the hot chocolate." She gave him a wink.

He didn't want to go back to the Hot Chocolate Fest or the Raven Lake Trail or the Frontier Freeze or the Reindeer Rodeo or the gingerbread contest. None of those things would ever be fun again without Holly.

There was some noise downstairs, and his

mom said something about someone being sick. Without any knocking, Oliver burst into his room. "Get up. We need to talk to my mother about what happened last night."

"Nothing happened last night."

"Well, that's not what we're going to say. We're going to say that I hired this woman to test him and he failed. You are going to say you were there and you saw it with your own eyes."

Jonah sat up in his bed. His anger gave him some energy. "He didn't fail, Oliver. You promised me that if he didn't fail, you were going to let this go."

"Listen to me, my mother is not marrying a Hayward. I don't care how faithful he was last night. He won't be once he gets a ring on that finger. I will not put her through that."

"Randall is not going to cheat on her."

"Randall, like the rest of his family, are a bunch of lowlifes. We aren't bringing these people into our lives."

Jonah swung his legs off the bed and got to his feet. "That's really not your decision to make. If Gran wants to spend the rest of her life with Randall, who are we to tell her she can't?"

"Fine, you don't want to be a witness, I don't need you. I have some semicompromising videos and pictures. You just stay up here while I break the news to her."

Oliver was out the door and down the stairs by the time Jonah had a chance to make it across the room to the door.

"Mom, we need to talk," Jonah heard Oliver say. "It's really important and I want you to know this is not how I wanted things to play out."

"What are you talking about?"

"I have some bad news about Randall."

Jonah wasn't going to let this nonsense go on. He joined them in the living room, where Gran was sitting on her settee reviewing her guest list. "Gran—"

"Jonah, you need to stay out of this," Oliver warned.

"I'm not going to stay out of it."

The doorbell rang and Jonah's mom offered to go answer it.

"There are a lot of reasons why you should stay out of it, son."

"I'm not your son, Oliver."

His uncle squared his shoulders and puffed out his chest.

"Randall," Gran said, her expression brightening the moment she laid eyes on him.

Jonah turned and saw Randall wasn't alone. A very solemn-looking Holly stood behind him. She winced when she saw Jonah.

"What brings you by, sweetheart?" Gran asked. "And Holly. Come on in here. What's going on?"

"Holly has something to tell you," he said. His tone was a little too gruff for Jonah's liking. "I'm glad Jonah is here because I think he has some things to say as well."

"Me?" He swallowed hard and glanced at Holly again. Her guilt was written all over her face. She must have come clean to Randall and he brought her over here to be honest with Gran.

"I think we should start with my information," Oliver said. "Maybe it's a good thing that Randall is here to answer for himself."

Oliver had no idea what he was doing. If Holly was going to spill her beans and Jonah was going to have to be honest about his part, Jonah was also going to be totally honest about Oliver's manipulation.

"I think Holly needs to tell your mother something first," Randall insisted.

"Why don't you tell my mother why you were flirting with this woman last night?" Oliver held out his phone with a picture of the woman in the pink jacket.

Randall squinted to get a better look. "Sarah?"

"Shari," Jonah corrected.

"That's what I said, Shari. What's she got to do with anything?"

"You were flirting with her yesterday at the Hot Chocolate Fest. She was actually working undercover for me and I have video and photos to prove that you cheated on my mother."

"You have video and pictures of me cheating on your mother? With Sarah?"

"Shari," Jonah corrected.

"That's what I said. We stood in the crowded square with my friends and your nephew. She came over with some friend of hers and they were talking to me. I told her it was nice meeting her, but that I was engaged when she asked me if I wanted to grab some real drinks with her alone. I declined."

"That's exactly what happened," Jonah confirmed. "She was doing her best to get him to take her somewhere private where they could be alone and he turned her down every time."

"Hold on a second. You hired this woman to hit on Randall?" Gran asked Oliver.

"Jonah and I wanted to make sure you knew who you were marrying. He's never had a committed relationship, Mom."

Randall's glare shifted to Jonah. "You were in on this? Holly said you were done trying to sabotage my wedding. Why would you get involved in this ridiculous scheme?"

"You were working with Oliver to make it look like Randall was cheating?" Holly asked, stepping farther into the room. "You did tell me you were done. You were so mad at me for still plotting with my dad."

"You were plotting what with your dad?" Clarissa asked.

Holly fiddled with her earring. "I didn't mail the invitations, Clarissa. It was part of a plan to get you to accuse me of stealing the invites so Randall would come to my defense and call off the wedding."

Gran's shoulders sagged and she covered her mouth with her hand in shock.

"I am so sorry, Clarissa. I was wrong and I need you to know that I felt terrible because I think you are a very nice person and I know you love Randall."

"But you were trying to get Randall to break up with me. You were trying to get me to break up with Randall," she said, pointing at Jonah. "I'm stunned. I expected something like this from Oliver, but you, Jonah. I didn't think you would do that to me."

"I didn't think Randall would cheat on you. The only reason I let Oliver go through with it was because I knew Randall would pass with flying colors. I had seen how you two care about each other. I knew he wouldn't risk it."

"That didn't stop you from trying to break us up earlier with Holly's help," Randall said.

Clarissa put her hand on her forehead. "My head is spinning."

"Do you want to know why Jonah and Holly have been trying to get us to go to events and spend time with us? It's not because they love us or even because they like each other. It's because they thought they could make the experience uncomfortable for one of us and we would cancel the wedding because we were incompatible."

"What? Jonah, please tell me that's not true."

Randall stared him down until he admitted the truth. "I'm sorry, Gran. I was caught up in the family feud and I thought I needed to prove to you that he couldn't fit in your world and that you couldn't fit in his. But you shocked us all. You two compromise and support one another. You are such a good role model for how to be successful when you don't always have the same interests."

The way Gran looked at him made him feel like a complete jerk. "I'm devastated. I don't know what to say."

"Doesn't anyone want to see the video of Randall and Shari?" Oliver asked, scrolling through his phone.

Jonah snatched his phone out of his hands and tossed it across the room. "No one wants to watch your fake video. Please stop."

"He doesn't deserve your politeness," Holly said, scowling at Oliver.

"You're going to judge me? When you and my nephew have been plotting and conniving all month long? Weren't you the one who got them kicked out of the Devonshire?"

Holly's lips pressed in a thin line and she closed her eyes, probably wishing she could teleport out of this house right now because that was how Jonah felt.

"You did what?" Randall snapped at Holly.

"We went back to the Devonshire after Gran and I met with the woman there. We basically asked some questions that made her think we were going to be a handful and she withdrew the offer to use the room."

"I can't believe you did that when you knew how much your grandmother wanted to have her wedding there." Randall didn't have to work very hard to shame Jonah. He felt all of it.

"We were misguided. I know saying we're sorry isn't enough, but we are," Jonah said, knowing they didn't deserve to be forgiven.

Gran wiped her eyes. "I... I don't believe what I'm hearing. I'm absolutely heartbroken."

Randall sat beside her and wrapped his arm around her while she sobbed quietly. Jonah's mom brought her some tissues.

Holly twisted her lips as she attempted to hold in her own tears. Jonah didn't know how to comfort her. He could only imagine how mad she was at him after he had laid into her about the invites and let her believe he was done with the games.

"They didn't want to come to our wedding so badly that they went to all this trouble to ruin it." Gran took Randall by the hand. "I guess there's only one thing to do."

"Gran." Jonah knew he had no defense for his actions, but he didn't want her to change her plans now. "Please don't cancel your wedding. I think it's safe to say that Holly and I don't want you to do that."

"I'm not canceling our wedding. There is nothing I want more than to marry Randall. We deserve this wedding given all the terrible things you have done to stop it. What I was going to say is since you all didn't want to come to our wedding, I am going to disinvite every last one of you. You are not welcome at the ceremony or the reception."

CHAPTER SEVENTEEN

JONAH HAD BEEN invited to several weddings, especially right after college and vet school. There was one summer he went to six. Sometimes he had wished he hadn't been invited, especially when he didn't know the couple very well. However, he had never been uninvited to a wedding. Until today.

Oliver thought it was appropriate to argue with his mother after everything he had done. He didn't want her to get married, but he was offended when she uninvited him.

Holly had tears streaming down her face. Jonah couldn't stand it any longer. "I'm going to take Holly home," he announced. He wasn't going to subject her to any more of this.

He put a hand on her arm and guided her to the door. When they were away from everyone else, he stopped and wrapped his arms around her and finally gave her the comfort he knew she needed.

"I'm sorry," he whispered.

"We deserved it."

"I know, but I'm still sorry you had to go through that."

She pressed herself against him and he allowed himself to take in the comfort she provided him as well. This cocoon was the only safe place in the world right now. They had nothing but messes to clean up everywhere else.

"I'm really mad at you," she said without moving.

He tightened his hold on her in case she got any ideas of running away. "I know. I should have told you what was happening last night. I was embarrassed that Oliver went to those lengths. I meant what I said. I only went through with it because I believed that Randall would pass his dumb test with flying colors. There was no chance he was going to disrespect my grandmother like that."

"He never would have."

"I wish we would have told them earlier

when we realized they weren't bad for each other."

"I wish I would have stood up to my dad earlier. I don't know why I put his feelings above everyone else's."

He really didn't want to let go, but he needed to look her in the eye. Her soft brown eyes that gave away the fact that she wasn't as tough as she wanted everyone to believe.

"You love your dad. You love your family, fiercely. That's one of the things I like about you."

"Even when it's the reason we can't be together?"

"Even then."

"Can you take me back to the Roadrunner? I need to talk to my sister and apologize to my mom."

He did as she asked. He let her go and took her back to the bar. He knew that things were going to go back to the way they were before Randall proposed to Gran. Back then, Jonah couldn't remember running into Holly anywhere. They didn't eat at the same places, they didn't go to the same stores, they didn't hang out with the same people.

They lived in the same small town and never saw one another.

That pain in his chest was back. His love-sickness reared its ugly head. He did not want things to go back to the way they were. He had no idea how to convince her of that, though.

He decided not to go home. He didn't want to face his grandmother or Randall. He certainly didn't want to see Oliver. He went to the clinic instead. There was always paperwork to look over, animals to check on. Work had always been his comfort place.

Dr. Lang was in the office this Saturday. He always had a full schedule on Saturdays. Dogs that ate things they shouldn't, cats that didn't want their shots, rabbits with strange viruses.

Mandy was surprised to see him when he walked in. "Dr. Drake, I thought you were taking the day off."

"I decided to come in and work on some paperwork. I won't be going out to see patients."

Mandy nodded and offered to get him a cup of coffee. She was the best office manager/receptionist they'd ever had. Jonah

entered his cramped office and slipped out
of his jacket and into his chair. A mountain
of files covered his desk. He had been distracted these last couple of weeks. There
was always somewhere to go or something
to do related to Randall and Gran. He had
been happy to go because he knew Holly
would be there.

"Here's some coffee," Mandy said. "Can
I get you anything else? Dr. Lang brought
in doughnuts. There might be a powdered
one left."

"I'm fine, Mandy. Thanks."

"There's a puppy."

"You want me to eat a puppy?"

Mandy's eyes went wide and then she
burst out laughing. "No! Not to eat. To cuddle or pet. She's adorable. There were five
of them. We were holding them until they
were adopted. We have one left, so we've
been taking turns keeping her company and
taking her home at night."

"If I feel the need to cuddle a puppy, I will
check it out."

"I know you're a horse guy, but dogs are
a man's best friend. And you look like you
could use one of those right now."

She left him alone. Alone. He was always alone. He lived with his mother and grandmother, but he was alone. It was a terrible feeling.

He tried to do some paperwork, but his thoughts were a jumbled mess. There was no way for him to keep things straight, not after everything that had happened today. Coming to work was a bad idea.

He got up and took his coffee cup to the break room. He washed it and put it back where it belonged. That was when he heard it. The tiny yapping from the kennels. There was a sadness in that yap, a sadness he felt in his bones. It was the same kind of sadness he was feeling right now. It was a lonely sadness.

There in the first kennel was the cutest ugly mutt he had ever seen in his whole life. She was definitely part terrier. Her gray-and-white fur stuck up in all directions. There was no rhyme or reason for where it was going. The best part was the little pink tongue that stuck out of her mouth like she was unable to rein it in.

"What's your name, little lady?"

She looked at him and the entire back end

of her body swung manically back and forth. This pup did not wag her tail—she wagged her whole body.

The card on the door read Holly Berry. "Is that your name? Holly Berry? I know someone else named Holly, but she doesn't want to be my friend right now. You, on the other hand, you look like you want to be my friend. Do you want to be my friend?" He opened the kennel door and Holly leaped into his arms. "I'll take that as a yes."

He carried her to the front. "Would it be okay if I took a turn with Holly Berry?"

"Of course. It looks like she really wants to go with you." Mandy laughed as Holly licked Jonah on the neck and cheek.

"I think she does."

Mandy helped him pack up some supplies. She gave him some food and a little leash. He walked out with his new little friend and immediately knew where he had to go. "I think you need to meet the other Holly in my life."

MAISY WASN'T TALKING to Holly or their dad. Her mom wasn't talking to her dad, but had a lot to say to Holly. Her dad wasn't talking to anyone. He was locked in his office. Frank had thankfully gone home.

Holly was behind the bar, making drinks but little conversation. She felt like the worst person in the world. Her favorite family member hated her guts. He didn't blink an eye when his wife-to-be uninvited her to the wedding.

She had no idea how she was going to make amends with anyone. Just like when she was nine years old and got in a fight with her mom about not wanting to wear a dress, the only option that made sense was running away. At thirty, she actually had some money that made a great escape possible.

Maisy put a ticket on the bar but didn't say a word before walking away. Holly slapped her hand over the ticket and pulled it toward her. She started on those drinks and did some math in her head. If she drove all night at seventy-five miles per hour, she could get about…*seventy-five times six, carry the three*…she had no idea. She could get out of Colorado at least.

"I don't think you can bring that in here."

"Aw, look at the puppy."

"It's so cute!"

Holly glanced up and Jonah was there holding the strangest-looking dog she'd ever seen.

"What are you doing?"

"Holly, this is Holly Berry. She's the last puppy in her litter and I didn't want to leave her alone, so I brought her home. You guys have the same name. I thought you might like to meet her."

"She's adorable… I think. She's kind of…"

"Ugly? I know. But she's the cutest ugly dog in the whole wide world. Look at her pink tongue. She can't make it stay in her mouth."

Holly reached across the bar and took the funny-looking dog in her arms. "Hey there, sweet girl. We have the same name. It's no wonder you were the last dog standing." She turned her attention back to Jonah. "Are you adopting her?"

"I think I might. I also think I might move out of my house. Out of my grandmother's house."

Holly tightened her hold on the puppy

for support. "Did she kick you out of the house?"

"No, no. Well, I guess that's a distinct possibility. I didn't go back home after I left here. I went to work. Moving is my idea. I think I had an epiphany. I don't have a life. I live in my grandmother's house. I work. I don't really have many friends. I imagine being a dad someday but I don't put myself out there and try to meet people, which is what I have to do in order to find someone who wants to be my wife and have children with me. I'm letting my life pass me by. I don't want to do that anymore. So, I'm going to adopt this dog and I'm going to get my own place, and I'm going to go out with friends, and I'm going to date someone who might want to marry me someday and have my children."

The confrontation today might have pushed him over the edge. "Should I be worried about you?"

"I want that person to be you, Holly. The one that I date. I want that to be you and I don't care what my last name is or your last name is or who hates us right now or any of that. I want to take you out to dinner and kiss you at the end of the night. I need you to not care about all those things and to want those other things, too. Can you do that?"

"Jonah." She let out a sigh.

"Don't *Jonah* me. Do you want those things?"

This wasn't as easy as saying yes or no. It was complicated and after today, wasn't it going to be more complicated? "I think we've been over this."

"Stop. I don't want to talk about what I deserve or you deserve. We are both imperfect people. I want to know if you want to go out to dinner with me. That's it. Let's start right there. Stop worrying about all the other stuff."

Could it be that simple? She stared at him for a minute. He had the best cheekbones for a guy and his nose had this bump that made her want to run her finger over it and pretend it was a skier on a ski jump. She knew he would laugh at that and not at all be self-conscious about it. He had these brown eyes that were the exact same color as hers. It was like looking in a mirror sometimes, but it was comforting at the same time.

If she stripped everything else away—

their names, all the family conflicts, their memories from high school—Jonah was exactly whom she wanted to go to dinner with.

"I do. I want to go to dinner with you."

The smile that broke across his face was worth everything she went through today. "We're going to figure everything else out. I promise you. With my brains and your guts, we are not only going to get reinvited to this wedding, but we're going to get your dad and my uncle to give toasts at the reception."

He had her up until that fantasy part there at the end. "I think your epiphany might have been more like a break from reality."

He was still smiling. "I am going to go home and start looking for my own place. I will call you soon to figure out when we can do that dinner. I need my dog back, though."

Holly gave Holly Berry a kiss on her cute/ugly head and handed her over. Maisy came over and crossed her arms over her chest.

"I want to see the dog."

Jonah obliged and Maisy turned into a puddle of mush just like she did when she was around babies. "You're such a good girl, aren't you? Yes, you are. Such a pretty girl."

"She's adorable, right?" Jonah asked.

Maisy's voice went from high-pitched and loving to dark and sinister. "I'm still so mad at you guys that I could scream, but I believe that you are going to do whatever it takes to make things right with Randall and your grandma. I know that you will find a way to keep this family from being destroyed even though you set off a giant bomb and tried to blow it to smithereens."

Holly was just happy she was talking to her again. "I'm going to fix this, Maisy. I promise."

"Yeah, well. You better." She held up the puppy and made a kissy face. The light and cheery voice was back. "And Jonah better take good care of you, sweet girl. Yes, he better." She handed the puppy back to Jonah and suddenly she sounded like an MMA fighter before a big match. "And you better take good care of my sister. I don't want to hear you two try to convince anyone that you don't belong together. Do you hear me?"

"I hear you."

"Where are the drinks for Table Five?"

Holly had been so distracted she hadn't finished. "Coming right up."

Maisy nodded and went to the kitchen pickup window to see if the food was ready.

"She's scary."

"She's pregnant. Do not mess with her when she's pregnant."

"Duly noted. Now, I'm leaving, but I'm going to call you tonight and we're going to do totally lame stuff like chat about our day and such. Is that cool?"

Holly laughed through her nose. "That is not even close to being cool. It's far, far away from cool, but I'm totally okay with doing that. I'll be waiting for that call."

Jonah left and Holly felt like *she* had an epiphany. They were going to make things right. They had one week and they were going to do everything to make sure that Randall and Clarissa had the best wedding ever.

CHAPTER EIGHTEEN

THE WEEK BEFORE Christmas was busy for a normal person, but the week before a Christmas wedding was off-the-charts busy. Holly had been working nonstop to make sure everything for the reception was perfect. Randall, of course, thought that Maisy was making sure that everything was perfect. Maisy and Bonnie were the only Haywards allowed to talk to Randall at the moment.

Randall and Clarissa had decided to still have the reception at the Roadrunner as long as Holly and Will were not within ten miles of it when the reception was going on. Bonnie promised that she would keep it Will and Holly-free on the day of the wedding, but she was more than willing to take Holly's help beforehand. Holly was holding out hope that she could somehow earn Randall's forgiveness before the big day. Time was running out.

It was Christmas Eve and everything had to be done today if tomorrow was going to go off without a hitch. There were place settings to arrange and centerpieces to put together. They needed to string some lights over the dance floor and unpack all the champagne flutes they had ordered to go along with bottles of champagne that would be on each table.

"What time is the food delivery coming?" Bonnie asked Holly while she was in the middle of counting napkin rings.

"Forty-six, forty-seven, forty-eight, forty-nine, fifty. Okay, we have just enough." Holly was standing at the bar. She jotted the number down on her inventory sheet. It was the only way she could keep it all straight. "The guy I spoke to said it would be here by four."

"Perfect. Maisy and I are going to get our nails done. We should be back by then." She left out the fact that it wasn't only her and Maisy. Bonnie, in an attempt at mending some fences, invited Clarissa, Nancy and any of the other ladies in the Drake family to get manicures if they wanted to join them. Clarissa said she would come as long as Holly was not there.

"I can stay until the food gets here. I can make sure the perishables get put away. That way everything will be ready when you get back. I was also thinking that maybe tomorrow I could help in the kitchen, manage the staff so everything gets out on time."

"That's very sweet of you, honey, but I promised Randall that you and dad wouldn't be anywhere near the reception on the night of. You understand, right?"

"I get it, Mom." It hurt like heck, but she understood why Randall didn't want her around. He had trusted her more than anyone else and she had betrayed him.

"Maisy, we've got to go or we're going to be late," Bonnie said as she threw on her coat. The two of them grabbed their purses and waved goodbye.

It was situations like this one that made her even more determined to make amends. She was going to show him and Clarissa that they didn't have to worry. Earning their trust back wasn't going to be easy, but she wasn't going to stop until it was done. It was one of the things that she and Jonah talked about on the phone every night.

Will came out of the back room. It took three days, but he was now talking to everyone in the family again. He hadn't gotten into any serious conversations with anyone other than their mom, but it was progress.

"Has anyone seen my phone? I set it down and now I can't find it," he asked as he scanned the bar top.

"I haven't seen it," Holly replied since she was the only person there to answer.

"Ah!" He spotted his phone next to the register. "Found it."

"Can I talk to you for a second?" she asked before he disappeared back into his office.

"What do you need, sweetheart?"

"I wanted to talk to you about the wedding."

He put his hands up. "I am not allowed to *think* about the wedding. Your mother has made it clear that if I so much as have a fleeting thought about doing anything to this wedding, she will leave me. I don't want your mother to leave me."

"I don't want Mom to leave you, either. I

am not going to make you do anything that would mess with the wedding. I've been trying to help so they see that I want to be a part of their day."

"The best way we can help is to stay far, far away."

Holly had one objective and that was to fix her family. These wounds weren't going to heal on their own. Will and Holly needed to be proactive. "Dad, you love Randall. I know that you want to make things right between the two of you. If we can show that we support this wedding, I think we'll be able to work things out."

"I don't even know how we got in this mess, honey. How am I supposed to get myself out?"

"We're in this mess because you and I put our feelings above Randall's," Holly said. "Not only did we not think about what he wanted, we didn't care what he wanted."

Will rubbed his bald head. "Exactly. We didn't listen. That's why we need to listen now. He said stay away and that's what I plan on doing."

Holly understood his reasoning but hated

not being able to make things right. "I'm not giving up yet."

Will put his hand on top of hers. "You know who I can make things right with? You. Your mother has pointed out to me that as the head of this family, I have a responsibility to you and your sister even as adults to be a positive role model. Instead of doing that, I asked you to lie and steal. I was a terrible dad."

"You're not a terrible dad."

"I was raised with this fear that the Drakes were going to take what's mine because that was what happened to my grandfather. I've been waiting for them to show up and steal what I've worked for. I taught you to fear them, too. I made you believe they were going to do us wrong. When Randall proposed to Clarissa, I guess I felt like instead of taking my bar or my house, they came for my uncle. My fear came true and I thought I needed to stop them."

That was exactly what happened. This hand-me-down grudge did nothing but create an irrational fear. "The Drakes are people just like us. They don't have some hidden agenda to stop us from succeeding. Refusing to interact with them or allow them to love the people we love doesn't do anything but take joy away from everyone."

Her phone rang, interrupting her. It was Jonah so she held up a finger to ask her dad to hang on a second before answering the call.

"Have you seen a horse give birth?"

"That is a very interesting way to start a conversation."

"Sorry. I should have started with hello. I miss you. Have you ever seen a horse give birth?"

Holly giggled. "Hello to you. I miss you, and I have never seen a horse giving birth before."

"We have a horse here on the ranch that's in labor. I thought maybe you'd like to hang out with me on foal watch."

"You're going to have a baby horse?"

"We are. And it's called a foal. That's why we're on foal watch."

His need to speak like a professional made it too hard to resist having some fun. "What's its ETA? Because I one hundred percent want to be on baby horse watch."

"There's no telling for sure, but the *foal* should be born sometime today."

"I'm coming over then as soon as I am done here." Holly ended the call and rested her chin on her hand.

"Randall's not the only one who wants to be with a Drake, is he?"

She knew she was wearing a dopey smile and it was a direct result of talking to Jonah. "He's not. But I've been pushing Jonah away because I didn't want to disappoint you or make you think I was choosing them instead of you. I don't want you to feel like me loving him would mean I would somehow stop loving you. My love is not land. It doesn't have a beginning or an end. It can grow."

"Yeah, I get that now. I want you to be happy, sweetheart. That's all I've ever wanted. I shouldn't be judging who you love. I should have told Randall the same thing."

"There's still time to make things right."

"The wedding is tomorrow. You might have to let this go."

Holly leaned in closer. "You wanna bet?"

"How's she doing?" Jonah asked Carter, whom he had left in charge of Annabelle while he took Holly Berry for a quick walk.

"Same. She's been getting up, lying down. She's feeling it."

Jonah could see that Annabelle was sweating around her neck. "Well, until her water breaks, she's going to be uncomfortable. I have a feeling I'm going to be here all night."

"I can stick around if you need me to," Carter offered.

"You need to go be with your family and enjoy your Christmas. I have someone coming to keep me company."

"Make sure they take some pictures of the foal. My kids would love to see them."

"Will do. Merry Christmas, Carter. Thanks for all you do around here."

"Merry Christmas, Dr. Drake. I'll see you at the wedding tomorrow."

Jonah didn't have the heart to explain he wasn't invited to his own grandmother's wedding, so he nodded and waved goodbye. Tensions were still high at the Drake ranch. Gran wasn't talking to him except to inform him that she didn't give him permission to bring a dog into her house. When he informed her and his mom he was thinking about finding his own place in town, she turned to her daughter-in-law and said, "It's about time."

She had every right to be angry. He had

purposely made her feel uncomfortable, been plotting behind her back, and sabotaged her wedding and reception plans for the Devonshire.

It didn't matter that he had truly believed he was protecting her. He had betrayed her trust and it wasn't something she would give him so easily the next time.

His phone pinged with a text. Holly was there and wondering where to find him. She didn't want to accidentally bump into his grandmother. He ran out of the stables to greet her.

"What in the world are you wearing?" she asked with a smile the size of Texas.

He knew she wasn't referring to his clothes because he had on jeans and a sweatshirt under his jacket. She was talking about the baby sling wrapped around his body so he could hold Holly Berry. He was a total sucker for this dog, but he didn't care.

"It's a sling. It lets me move around and do things with two hands while still holding Holly Berry. She likes being held. All. Day. Long."

Holly laughed. "You cannot hold that dog

all day every day. She needs to learn to be an independent female."

"She's just a baby right now. Don't make me grow her up too quickly."

Holly shook her head as she stepped close and bent down to give the dog a kiss on the head before kissing him on the cheek. "You are such a softie. How's the baby horse–watching going?"

He knew she was refusing to say *foal* on purpose. "No foal yet. Come to the stable and you can see for yourself."

"How long will she be in labor?"

"Could be an hour, could be four. I'm not sure how she's feeling. She might hang on so she can have a Christmas baby or give up and let it happen Christmas Eve."

"It's not like she has a choice."

"I've seen a lot of horses give birth. The mare often tends to do it in the middle of the night. Not to say there are some that come first thing in the morning or whatever, but a large number of them wait to have their foal when it's late at night and everything is dark and quiet."

"Seriously?"

"Some think it's an instinctual thing. When

horses were wild, the nighttime offered them some protection from predators during the birthing process."

"You know I'm starting to find your nerd talk very attractive. I'm not sure how that happened."

"What if I tell you that to promote healthy circadian rhythms in the foal, it helps to have proper melatonin levels."

"I have absolutely no idea what that means, but I totally want to make out with you right now."

Jonah brushed some hair from her face and leaned in to kiss her smiling lips. She was careful not to smush Holly Berry, but she wasn't quick to pull away. He was going to make sure to use all his fancy words from now on.

"You wouldn't believe how much that used to annoy me. I must really like you," she said.

"I'm glad you do."

The crunching of gravel caught their attention. Randall's car pulled up to the house. Holly immediately tensed. He got out and eyed them both suspiciously.

"Seeing you two together here makes me

nothing but nervous. If you think you're going to spoil something this close to our wedding day, I won't have it."

"We're not here to spoil anything," Holly said.

"Annabelle is foaling. Holly came to keep me company while we wait for it to be born."

Randall seemed to relax ever so slightly. "You have a new foal coming tonight?"

"She's been in labor a couple hours. We're waiting for her water to break, then things will move along quickly."

"Since when are you interested in seeing horses give birth?" he asked Holly.

"Since I started dating a guy who takes care of horses that give birth."

Randall nodded; his lips were firmly pressed in a straight line. "You should be careful. I hear there are some people in this town who don't think Drakes and Haywards should be allowed to be happy together and will go to some wild lengths to see to it that they can't be."

"We were wrong, Uncle Randall. I don't think I'll ever forgive myself for what I did to you guys."

"That makes two of us," he replied sadly. He turned and headed for the house.

Jonah could tell that cut deep. Holly looked totally dejected.

"Hey, Randall!" he called out. "Do you want to know when the foal is coming?"

Randall stopped and glanced over his shoulder. "I'm sure your grandmother would like that."

"We still have a chance," Jonah whispered. He took Holly by the hand and brought her back to the stables. "That's the most he's talked to me this whole week, and he's willing to come out here to watch the foaling with us. That's progress."

"He hates me."

"He loves you. If he hated you, he wouldn't care."

She walked over to Annabelle's stall. The horse was lying down and Jonah noticed that her water had broken.

"Won't be long now." He opened the door to her stall and took a closer look. "We should probably have Gran and Randall come out if they want to watch. Do you want to call him?"

Holly got on her phone and let them know

it was time. Annabelle was on her side in the pile of hay. She raised her head to look at her stomach. He knew she was ready for this to be over.

"You're doing a good job, Annabelle."

Jonah could see the white amniotic sac and the foal's legs beginning to emerge.

"What can I do to help?" Holly asked.

Jonah handed her Holly Berry. "Can you hold her? Annabelle needs my full attention."

Holly cradled his dog in her arms and watched intently as Jonah went over to help Annabelle push the foal out. Randall and Gran appeared and peeked into the stall.

"That was fast," Randall said.

"I thought for sure she'd do this on our wedding day. Just to add to the chaos," Gran said to Randall.

"Randall, do you want to come help me?" Jonah asked as he tugged on the foal's legs.

Randall entered the stall and got down on one knee. The two men worked together to bring the foal all the way out. Jonah carefully pulled away the sac and rubbed the foal's nose to clear out its muzzle. The little foal jerked its head around.

"Gran, can you hand us those towels on the bench?"

Randall and Jonah wiped the foal down and then tucked it in with fresh hay to keep it warm. Annabelle turned herself around and started licking her baby clean like a good mama did. Her soft nickering let her foal know she was there for it.

"Is it a boy or a girl?" Holly asked.

"It's a colt," Randall announced.

Gran clapped. She had been hoping for a male. "Good job, Annabelle. You did good."

Annabelle kept on licking her little colt as he started moving, doing his best to get to his feet. Jonah helped him get his feet under him. The colt tried and failed to stand but remained determined. Another try and he was up on his four wobbly legs. He took an uneasy step before flopping down.

Jonah helped position him again. "You got this, little buddy. You can do it."

The colt got up and tried to stand still for a minute, his small brown body shivering under the fluorescent lights in the stable.

"I can't believe they just get up and walk right after they're born," Holly said, clearly in awe of what she just witnessed.

"Horses are pretty incredible," Gran said.

"Did you guys have names picked out ahead of time?" Holly asked.

"I've been so busy, I haven't been thinking about Annabelle having a foal. What do you think, Randall?"

"We should give it a name that has something to do with Christmas, don't you think? Holly, what was the name of that dog your grandpa gave your grandma on Christmas that one year? Do you remember? It was white and had brown spots."

"Dash?"

"Was that his name? I thought it was more Christmassy than that."

"He was Dasher, but we all called him Dash."

"That's right. He was named after the reindeer, which is perfect for a Christmas Eve, given that's when the reindeer do their stuff. Dasher is a good horse name. If he's fast, it will be a good fit," Randall said. "What do you think, Clarissa?"

Gran wrung her hands. "I kind of like the name Comet better. What do you think about that?"

"I think Comet is a great horse name. If

he's fast, it will also be a good fit," Randall said with a wink. Seeing the way Randall made her feel okay about making her own decisions made Jonah feel like a bigger heel. Randall was the right man for her.

"Comet it is," Jonah said. "He looks good. I'm going to finish taking care of Annabelle and then I'll get him set up to start nursing. Holly, don't let me forget to take some pictures for Carter. His kids wanted to see Comet."

"That's good of you," Gran said. "Thank you, Jonah, for taking care of Annabelle and Comet."

"No problem, Gran. I'm happy to help."

She nodded.

"You got this? Do you need my help?" Randall asked.

"I've got it. Maybe you could take Holly Berry inside for me. She's got to be ready for bed. Her crate is in my room."

Gran took the puppy from Holly. "You're going to have to change this dog's name if you're going to be spending more time with human Holly. You'll confuse it."

"I'll take that into consideration," Jonah replied as Randall stepped out of the stall.

"Clarissa." Holly's voice cracked. "I know you're disappointed and angry with us, but when we started, we thought we knew better than you did. That arrogance blinded us at first to the amazing love you and Randall share. But it didn't take us long to see it. It became so clear to us that we were fighting a losing battle, we stopped fighting each other and were able to open our own hearts. That's how big your love is. I wanted you to know that I'm sorry I had to put you through everything we put you through to figure it out."

Again, Gran nodded, obviously too choked up to speak.

"Since we won't be seeing you two tomorrow," Randall said, backing away, "merry Christmas."

CHAPTER NINETEEN

CHRISTMAS DAY. HOLLY HAD never dreaded a Christmas before. This one was different. Today, her mom and her sister were going to a wedding. They were going to love and support Uncle Randall on his special day while Holly and her dad sat at home, feeling sorry for themselves.

The morning was spent at Maisy and Danny's, watching the kids open their presents and exchanging a few between the grown-ups. Holly tried to enjoy it, but thoughts about missing the impending nuptials kept nagging at her.

"We're going to head home so I can get ready for the wedding," her mom said, kissing her cheek. "Whatever you do at the Roadrunner today, thank you. Just make sure you're out of there before the wedding party arrives."

"I got it, Mom. I know I'm not invited. You don't have to keep reminding me."

"I'm sorry. I love you."

"I love you, too."

Holly and her dad waved to each other as he followed her mom out. They had plans to meet at the bar to make sure the place looked perfect for the reception.

"Thank you for the gifts. The kids are going to have a blast with those Legos," Maisy said.

The floor in the family room was littered with torn pieces of colorful wrapping paper. Danny had tried his best to keep up with it, but once the adults joined the kids in the unwrapping, it became impossible.

"Can I help you clean up?" Holly asked. "I know you need to get ready for the wedding."

Her sister waved her hand dismissively. "I got it. Don't worry."

"I guess we can talk tomorrow. You can tell me all about how things went."

"I'm sorry you can't come with us. You know I want you to be there. Who's going to dance with me all night? You know Danny's only good for one song."

Danny came walking out of the kitchen with a pancake in hand. "What about me and one song?"

"You're going to have to dance with me for more than one song tonight since Holly isn't going to be there."

"Thanks a lot, Holly. Why did you have to punish me?"

She cracked a half smile. "Sorry, big guy. I suggest wearing comfortable shoes so you don't get a blister from getting your groove on all night."

"I do one slow dance, Maisy. You know this."

Both women laughed, knowing Danny would do whatever his pregnant wife asked of him.

"I'll call you tomorrow and give you all the gossip."

"You can text me throughout the evening if you want as well."

Maisy promised to keep her in the loop as much as possible. Holly left her sister's and went straight to the Roadrunner. She had done everything she could yesterday to have it ready for today. The theme was Silver Bells. Everything was white and silver.

They had strung twinkling white lights back and forth across the length of the whole bar. The tables were draped in white with silver pillar candles on each one.

Randall had asked her to buy these little silver bells for people to ring instead of having guests clink their glasses to encourage the happy couple to kiss. Holly had found some that doubled as place card holders.

Those cardboard stars that had been hanging from the ceiling had been taken down and replaced with white glittery snowflakes. Holly also hung some on the walls.

The place looked spectacular. Hopefully Randall would feel her love in her attention to detail. Maisy had promised to tell him it was all her gift to him.

"Wow, this place looks amazing." Jonah was exactly what she needed right now, and there he was, holding a large box wrapped in red-and-green polka-dotted paper.

"How did you know I needed you?"

"I had a hunch." He looked so dapper today. Perhaps he had just come from church. He had on a charcoal-colored suit. His patterned tie had little Christmas trees all over it.

"I hate today. Can we skip to tomorrow?"

"I wish. But if we skip today, we'll miss the wedding."

Holly scrunched up her face in confusion. "We aren't invited."

"Yeah, I know." Jonah handed her the present. "This is for you."

Holly felt bad. She didn't have a present for him. So much had been going on, gift buying wasn't on her list of things to do this week. She carefully unwrapped the box and lifted the lid. Inside was a Christmas-red dress.

"You bought me a dress?"

Jonah wore a lopsided grin. "I did. You're going to need it."

"For what?"

"We're crashing the wedding."

IT WAS A risky move, but Jonah was determined to see his grandmother get married. He knew that if he presented Holly with the chance, she'd take it and they would figure it out together.

"What if we get there and they kick us out?" Holly asked. "That would be pretty humiliating."

"What if we go and they don't kick us out

because they realize they wanted us there and we have a great time?"

Holly took a deep breath and blew out the air slowly. "I don't want to do anything that could spoil their day. I want them to have no drama."

"We're not going to cause any drama. We want to be there to show them that we love them and that we're happy for them."

Holly began to pace and bite her fingernail. "They made it pretty clear they didn't want to see us today."

Gran hadn't said she didn't want to see them. She had thanked him. She wasn't as angry as she had been. She was beginning to open up to the idea of forgiving him and Holly.

"I think we need to try. I bet…we make it through the whole night."

She halted her pacing. "You wanna bet?"

"That's what I said, isn't it? I bet you that we make it through the whole night without getting kicked out."

"You're on." She took her dress in the back to get ready. They were going to the wedding.

Jonah wasn't expecting to be completely

blown away when Holly stepped back out, but he was rendered speechless when he saw her. The dress was a perfect fit thanks to Maisy. She hadn't known why he was asking for her sister's dress size. She was going to be as surprised as the rest of them.

"You are an excellent shopper. This dress is beautiful."

"You're beautiful."

"We're going to need a plan. Are we just walking in even though we weren't invited? Do we let them see us or do we hide in the shadows?"

Jonah liked that she put her hair up. It helped accentuate her neck. He wanted to kiss her in that dip where her neck ended and her shoulder began.

Holly snapped her fingers in front of his face. "Jonah, we need to have a plan."

"I think we go. We wait until everyone is in there. Then we take a seat in the back. By the time Gran or Randall notices us, it will be too late. They won't want to ruin it by calling us out."

"What about my dad?"

"What do you mean?"

"I can't go to the wedding and leave my dad here alone."

Jonah shrugged. No reason to leave a man behind. "We can see if he wants to come with us."

Will Hayward hadn't worn a suit since his daughter got married seven years ago. Will also wasn't on the same diet that his wife put him on before their daughter's wedding. This led to some challenges in getting him ready to crash the wedding.

"Those are not going to work," Holly said as soon as he came out in his suit coat and dress pants. "You can keep the suit coat but don't try to button it. Just let it hang open. Do you have any khakis?"

Will groaned and slipped back into his bedroom. When he came out a second time, Holly gave her approval.

"When we get there, we need to be discreet and just take our seats. Don't chitchat with anyone. Any questions?" Jonah asked once they were all in his truck.

Will raised his hand. "Can I sit by my wife?"

"No."

"Why not?"

"Because we are crashing this wedding. That means we need to maintain a low profile," Jonah explained.

Holly raised her hand. "What about Oliver?"

"What about Oliver?"

"Don't we need to bring Oliver? I think to be fair, we're going to have to ask him."

Jonah shook his head. "We are not bringing Oliver. He will get us kicked out for sure."

"No one probably likes Oliver less than I do, but this is his mother's wedding day," Holly said.

"I probably like him less," Will argued.

Holly nodded. "You've known him longer so that makes sense."

"Can you two stop?" Jonah sighed. "We can go ask him if he wants to come, but if he says no, we're going to accept that and move on, right?"

"Right," Holly and Will said in unison.

That was how the four of them ended up scrunched in the cab of his truck, driving to the ranch, ready to crash a wedding.

"What if they don't let us in?" Oliver

asked as they turned onto the road that led to the house.

"They didn't hire guards to man the door. We're going to walk in and discreetly sit in the back," Jonah said, looking for a spot to park among the other guests.

He helped Holly out of the truck once they were parked. "If someone asks us to leave, do not get confrontational. We leave. We've done enough to cause problems for Randall and Clarissa. We will not cause any more," she said to her wedding companions. "Understand?"

Everyone nodded.

They followed the little signs that Gran and Jonah's mom had handmade to guide the guests to the barn. When they got there, Gran was standing outside. She spotted them before they had a chance to hide.

"Jonah? Oliver? What in the world?"

"Gran, don't get mad. We are here because we love you and our hearts were so heavy, knowing you were going to get married without us here to show our love and support for you. If you want us to go, we will go. If you allow us to stay, we promise that we come in love and peace only."

"Is that how you really feel, Oliver?" she asked her son.

"I was a bonehead about all this, Mom. I thought I was doing what Dad would have wanted me to do. He would have hated the thought of you loving anyone but him and to top it off, it was a Hayward? He would have lost his mind." Oliver's eyes welled with tears. "But Dad left us a long time ago and I've watched you be alone for over a decade. As unhappy as Dad would be about all this, I believe he would never begrudge you the chance to be happy. I think that's why all my plans and all of their plans were foiled. You deserve to be happy, Mom."

Gran threw her arms around Oliver. Jonah wanted to hug him, too. He had said exactly what Gran had needed to hear.

"Thank you, son. You have no idea how much I needed to hear that right now. I've been feeling so sad all day, knowing that my family wasn't whole. I was standing out here wondering if I should postpone when I saw you four walk up. It was like the good Lord sent me a sign that it was going to be all right."

"Does that mean we get to go in?" Will asked.

"Please," she replied. "Except for Oliver."

Oliver's brow furrowed. "Why not me?"

"I need someone to walk me down the aisle and give me away. Do you think you can handle that?"

Relief relaxed his shoulders and his expression shifted to pride. "I can handle that."

Holly took Jonah's arm and they entered the barn ahead of the bride and her escort. Music began to play from somewhere. This wasn't the entrance Jonah had planned for. All of the guests were expecting his grandmother. Instead, they were getting a last-minute bridesmaid and a couple of groomsmen.

Randall stood with his head slightly tilted to the side at the end of the aisle. He was confused but not as surprised by these last-minute arrivals as Jonah would have expected. When they got to him, Holly reached for his hand.

"Please let us be part of your day. We come only to show our love and support," she whispered. It had worked for Jonah, but would Randall be as forgiving?

Will stepped up as well. "Please, Randall."

"You're blocking my view of the bride," Randall said. "You two need to stand over here and Holly, you need to stand there."

Jonah watched as a grateful smile lit up Holly's face. They took their places up front and joined the rest of their friends and family as Gran and Oliver came down the aisle. Gran looked radiant and Randall had to wipe his eyes as she got closer.

Oliver shook hands with Randall before giving the bride away. There wasn't a dry eye in the place. Jonah glanced over at Holly, who looked like the weight of the world had finally lifted off her shoulders. He was going to marry her someday. If Randall and Gran could do it, so could they.

The evening ended at the Roadrunner where all of this had started. The place thankfully didn't look or smell the way it did that first night, but Jonah was once again taken by the beauty of the woman who was usually behind the bar.

Tonight, she was in his arms on the dance floor. It had been a wild three weeks. In less than a month, Jonah's whole life had changed. He was going to find his own place, he had a girlfriend and he was the owner of the cutest ugly dog in Colorado. There was so much to be thankful for on this Christmas Day.

"I guess I lost the bet," Holly said as they swayed from side to side.

"We did not get kicked out."

"We did not. I am very happy to lose that bet."

"I am very happy to be here with you."

"We shouldn't stay too late. You have a puppy to get home to."

"This is true. I forgot to tell you that I changed her name. I think Gran was right. I don't want to confuse her when I constantly talk to her about my amazing girlfriend Holly."

"Is that right? What did you decide to name her?"

"Well, I wanted to stick to the holiday theme and I wanted her to still remind me of you since that's what prompted me to get her in the first place."

"Okay... So what's her name?"

"Ginger."

He expected the confused look on her face. "Ginger?"

"Like gingerbread because the gingerbread contest was where I am fairly certain I started to fall in love with you, Holly Hayward."

"That early, huh?"

"I'm a smart guy, remember. I know when something special is staring me in the face. I think that makes me the big winner."

"Well, for your information, I started falling for you at the tree lighting, so actually I'm the big winner because I started falling in love first."

He tickled her side and her laugh filled his heart with even more joy. "You cannot make that into a competition."

"I just did."

"Of course you did. But I think that means we're both the big winners."

Holly linked her arms around his neck and kissed him in front of everyone on the dance floor. "Hearts are breaking all over Coyote tonight," she said. "Coyote's most eligible bachelor is officially off the market."

"I love you, Holly."

And in typical Holly fashion, she replied, "I bet I love you more."

* * * * *